MASON WOLFE

WOLFE BROTHERS SERIES, BOOK THREE

SANDI LYNN

SANDI LYNN ROMANCE, LLC

MASON WOLFE

(WOLFE BROTHER'S SERIES, BOOK THREE)

New York Times, USA Today & Wall Street Journal
Bestselling Author
Sandi Lynn

Mason Wolfe

Copyright © 2020 Sandi Lynn Romance, LLC

Cover Photo by Wander Aguiar
Model: Andrew Biernat

❀ Created with Vellum

MISSION STATEMENT

Sandi Lynn Romance

Providing readers with romance novels that will whisk them away
to another world and from the daily grind of life – one book at a time.

CHAPTER 1

Mason

Chaos surrounded the area, but that didn't stop me from hearing the screams of a familiar voice.

"My baby. Where's my baby?" Mrs. Kent screamed as she looked around the area.

"Mrs. Kent. Where's Olivia?" I ran over to her and shouted as I gripped her shoulders.

She stood there in shock, blankly staring at me while tears flooded down her face.

"I just ran to the corner store. I was only gone for ten minutes."

"Mrs. Kent, is Olivia still in the apartment?" I shouted.

"Yes!" she screamed.

I grabbed my axe, ran inside the building and up six flights of stairs. Dense smoke infiltrated the air, keeping visibility low. Kicking in the door to apartment 6C, I screamed for Olivia as I ran down the narrow hallway.

"I'm in here." I heard a voice coming from the door on the left.

Opening it, I found her crouched in the corner.

"Mason, is that you?"

"Yeah, kid." I smiled as I bent down. "Let's get you out of here. Your

Mom is waiting for you outside."

"I'm too scared to move."

"I know, Olivia, but I'll protect you."

I grabbed the small towel sitting on her nightstand and had her cover her nose and mouth. Picking her up, her arms wrapped tightly around my neck. As I stepped out the door and into the hallway, flames engulfed the area around us, and the ceiling began to collapse.

"Captain, are you there?" I heard Bobbie's voice over the radio.

"Bobbie, I'm on the sixth floor and the ceiling is collapsing. I can't get to the stairs. We're trapped in here."

I took Olivia back inside the apartment as my mind raced. Looking straight ahead at the window, it was the only option I had.

"Mason, get the hell out of there now," Bobbie said.

"Get the air cushion ready. The only option I have is through the window. I repeat, get the air cushion ready now."

"We can bring the ladder as close to the building as possible," Bobbie spoke.

"There's no time. The ceiling is about to collapse inside the apartment. Get the air cushion ready now. That's an order."

I set Olivia down, and she refused to let go of me.

"Olivia, I need you to listen. Keep the towel over your face. I need to break the window."

"No." Her eyes widened as she shook her head. "No."

"We don't have a choice. I need you to trust me."

Particles fell from the ceiling as the cracking sounds alerted me there was no more time to waste.

"Bobbie, I'm breaking the window. Is that cushion ready?"

Taking my axe, I swung it at the glass as it shattered, and the noise of the cracking ceiling heightened.

"Captain, the air cushion is in place and ready. Get the hell out of there now!"

Grabbing a blanket from the couch, I wrapped it around Olivia and picked her up.

"Time to go, kid. Close your eyes as tight as you can and don't let go of me. I've got you."

Holding her securely in my arms, the ceiling collapsed, and flames engulfed the apartment as I jumped out the window with a ten-year-old girl in my arms. The moment we hit the air cushion, rescue teams came running over as did Olivia's mother.

"You saved my daughter. Thank you, Mason." Tears flowed down her face as she hugged Olivia tight.

"You okay?" Bobbie asked as he helped me up.

"I'm fine."

"Uh, you might not be in a minute." He laughed as he patted my shoulder.

I took off my helmet as I saw Nathan and my mother run towards me.

"Mason Matthew Wolfe!" she scolded as she gripped my arms. "Are you crazy?"

"Bro, that was outstanding!" Nathan grinned.

"Mom, what are you doing here?"

"We were on our way back from dinner when we saw the building fire. I nearly had a heart attack."

"Yeah." I sighed as I turned around and looked at my building, knowing everything I owned was engulfed in flames.

"You'll stay with me," my mom said as she placed her hand on my cheek. "And we will have a little talk about finding you another job."

"Mom, Mason will stay with me and Allison. We have some brotherly catching up to do. He's fine. Let him do his job. You can grill him about his heroic adventures another time." He hooked his arm around her.

"Thank you." I mouthed.

He gave me a thumbs up as he led her back to the cab. Walking over to where Olivia was being examined in the back of an ambulance, I took hold of her hand.

"You okay?" I asked with a smile.

"I'm okay. They're taking me to the hospital for a checkup. I get to ride in the back of this ambulance." Her eyes lit up.

"Cool, Olivia." I held my hand up for a high five.

"Thanks, Mason. Thanks for saving me. I didn't think we would

3

get out."

"Nah." I waved my hand. "I always get out." I gave her a wink. "Do you have somewhere you and Olivia can go?" I asked Mrs. Kent.

"I called my sister and she's meeting us at the hospital. How did this happen?"

"I don't know yet, but I will find out."

❧

*A*s I was standing in the shower, the only thing I could think about was how everything I owned was gone. The only possessions I had were packed in the bag I kept at the station. As I stepped out of the shower and wrapped a towel around my waist, Bobbie walked in.

"Your brother is here to see you."

"Which one?"

"Elijah. He's waiting for you in the kitchen."

"Tell him I'll be right out."

Throwing on some clothes, I walked to the kitchen.

"You okay?" Elijah smiled as he lightly hugged me.

"I'm fine. Let me guess, Mom called you?"

"Actually, Nathan called. He told me you jumped out of a six-story window with a child, Mom saw, and now she's freaking the fuck out on him."

"Of all the fires she had to be at." I shook my head as I grabbed two beers from the fridge and handed him one.

"She'll get over it. You're staying with Nathan until you find another place?"

"Yeah. Mom wanted me to stay with her."

"Ouch. Not a good idea. She'd have you chained to the house to keep you from going to work." He smirked.

"No shit." I let out a sigh.

"Thanks for the beer. I better get going. I just wanted to come by and make sure you were okay."

"Thanks, bro. I appreciate it." I gave him a hug.

CHAPTER 2

ason

I'd spent the night at the firehouse and once the sun rose the next morning, I grabbed my bag and headed to Nathan's. I'd felt like I was stuck in a nightmare and couldn't wake up. The events of last night took its toll on me knowing everything I owned was reduced to a pile of ashes.

"Just in time for breakfast." Nathan grinned as he opened the door.

Stepping inside, I set my bag down as Ruby came running into the foyer.

"Uncle Mason!" She threw her arms around me. "Dad told me you're staying with us."

"Yeah, Ruby. For a little while at least."

"I'm sorry about your apartment." Her mouth formed a pout.

"Thanks, kid. Me too." I sighed.

"Come on. Allison made French toast and eggs." Nathan patted my back.

Walking into the kitchen, Allison gave me a sympathetic look and a hug.

"Are you okay?"

"I'm fine, Allison. Thanks for letting me crash here."

"Don't be silly. You're always welcome here. Go sit down and I'll pour you a cup of coffee."

"Bro, I need to warn—" Nathan spoke.

"Good morning!" My mother's voice echoed through the house.

"Mom said she was coming over this morning." He sighed.

"Great. And you couldn't start with that the second I walked in?"

"There you are," she spoke as she walked over and gave me a hug.

"Morning, Mom."

"Let me look at you." She firmly planted her hands on each side of my face, and I heard Nathan snicker.

"Mom, I'm fine. You saw that I was fine last night."

"It was dark, Mason." She examined my face.

"Coffee, Caitlin?" Allison asked.

"Coffee sounds great, darling. Thank you." She took the empty chair next to me. "I was up all night worried sick about you. Mason, you really need to consider another line of work."

Here we go again.

"Mom, I love you, but you need to stop. I've been doing this for years. For god sakes, I'm a captain. Do you know how rare that is at my age? You should be proud of me."

"I am proud of you, darling. But being a firefighter is dangerous and seeing what I saw last night, well, it freaked me out even more."

"And I'm sorry about that, but all you're seeing are scary fires. You're not seeing the complete picture. I save people's lives, Mom. I saved that little girl's life last night."

"At the expense of yours," she spoke. "I love you, Mason. You boys are my entire world and I will not lose you."

I reached over and placed my hand on hers, for I understood where she was coming from.

"You will not lose me. Are you going to help me out here?" I glanced over at Nathan.

"Mom, leave him alone. He's doing a job he loves. A job that gives him purpose. Just like me, Elijah, and yourself. Being a lawyer is your life. You need to understand that being a firefighter is Mason's."

"You don't seem too worried about Nathan being a pilot. He could crash the plane," I spoke.

"Hey." Nathan furrowed his brows.

"I do worry about that sometimes, but you run into burning buildings every day. The risk is way higher. Anyway, I said what I needed to, and now I have to get to the office."

"You didn't finish your coffee," I said.

"Mom, it's Saturday," Nathan spoke.

"What's your point, darling?" She got up from her seat and kissed my cheek. "Take into consideration the stress you're putting your mother under."

"I'll walk you to the door, Grandma." Ruby smiled as she grabbed her hand.

Looking over at Nathan, I slowly shook my head as he sat there with a smirk on his face. Suddenly, we heard Ruby scream and a loud thump. Jumping up from my seat, I ran into the foyer and found my mother lying on the floor.

"Mom!" I knelt down beside her.

"Grandma, wake up!" Ruby yelled as Allison grabbed her and held her.

Pulling my phone from my pocket, I called 911.

"This is Captain Mason Wolfe from station 53. I need an ambulance at 40 Sullivan Street, now!"

"Mom," Nathan spoke as she came to.

"Don't move, Mom. The ambulance is on its way."

"What happened?" she groggily asked.

"You fainted. That's what happened," Nathan said.

"I'm fine." She went to get up, and I immediately stopped her.

"You are not to move," I spoke as I checked her eyes.

"Don't be ridiculous. I'm fine, and I'm not going to the hospital. I have to get to the office."

"Yes, you are. People just don't pass out for no reason. You're going to the hospital and having a doctor check you out."

I rode in the ambulance with her and listened while she said a few choice words to me. Nathan called Elijah and the two of them met us at the Emergency Room.

"Hey, Mason. You're not in uniform." Corinne smiled.

"Day off. My mom was just brought in."

"Oh no. I hope she's okay."

"She's fine right now. We've been waiting a while. Do you know which doctor she'll be seeing?"

"Let me check," she spoke as she typed away on her computer. "Dr. Davis."

"Ah, never heard of him. He must be new?"

"He is a she, and yes, she just started last week."

"Great. Thanks." I tapped the counter and headed back into my mother's room.

"Hey, Mason." Jason smiled as he walked in. "Not working today?"

"No. Not today. What are you still doing here? You usually work nights."

"I'm pulling a double because Lisa called in. By the way, I had a patient in here last night who wouldn't stop raving about you. A ten-year-old little girl you saved," he spoke as he poked my mother's arm with the needle.

"Ouch. Young man, watch it with that thing."

"Sorry, Ms. Wolfe." He smiled at her. "She told me the two of you jumped out a window from her six-story apartment."

"Just another day on the job," I spoke.

"Good morning," I heard a voice speak. "I'm Dr. Sara Davis."

I turned my head and for a split moment, our eyes locked, and I stood there speechless.

CHAPTER 3

*S*ara

"Wow. You have quite a gathering in here." I smiled as I stood and stared at the three sexy men in the room.

"These are my sons: Elijah, Nathan, and Mason."

I said hello to each of them and swallowed hard as Mason extended his hand to me.

"Nice to meet you, Dr. Sara Davis." The corners of his mouth curved upward.

"And you as well." I gently placed my hand in his. "So, tell me what happened."

"Nothing really. My boys are overreacting as usual."

"She fainted in the foyer of my home," Nathan said.

"Have you ever fainted before?" I asked her.

"Only when I was pregnant."

"Mom!" All three boys gasped.

"Settle down. I'm not pregnant for god sakes."

Taking my stethoscope, I listened to her heart and then proceeded with more of the exam.

"I'm starting you on an IV because you are a little dehydrated. Have you been eating and drinking okay?"

"Sure," she spoke, but I could sense a nervousness in her voice.

"Your blood pressure is a little high. Not too much, but higher than I'd like to see it. I'll go see if I can push that bloodwork through so we can find out what's going on. I'll be back in once I have the results."

"Thank you, Dr. Davis."

"You're welcome. If you need anything or feel unwell, just press the call button for the nurse." I gave her a smile as I walked out of the room.

I set my iPad down at the nurses' station and began typing my notes.

"So, I've never seen you here before."

With a slight turn of my head, my eyes fixated on Mason who was leaning up against the nurses' station. He had a look in his eyes. A look I knew all too well.

"Is that the best pickup line you can come up with?" I asked as I continued typing my notes.

"It's not a pickup line. It's a fact because I'm in here a lot. I'm Captain Mason Wolfe of the New York Fire Department, Station 53."

"You're a firefighter?" I cocked my head.

"I am. If you don't believe me, just ask Corinne." He gestured with his hand.

I raised my brow at Corinne, who sat there like a lost puppy begging to be taken home.

"Yes." She snapped back to reality. "He's a firefighter. Captain fire-fighter." She swooned as she bit down on her bottom lip.

"See. It wasn't a pickup line." The corners of his mouth curved upward.

"I'm new here, hence the reason you haven't seen me before. Now if you'll excuse me, I have work to do." I picked up my iPad and began to walk away.

"I'd like to buy you a drink sometime," he said as he followed behind me. "Preferably tonight. I can promise you'll have the best time of your life."

I stopped dead in my tracks with my iPad held tightly against my chest.

"I have plans tonight," I spoke as I turned around. "And before you say tomorrow night or the next night or even next week, I'm afraid I'm busy."

I walked away, but he still was following me. I could hear the "I won't take no for an answer" in his footsteps.

"Really? So basically what you're saying is you don't want to have drinks with me, ever. Am I right?"

"You are correct, Mr. Wolfe. Now if you'll excuse me, I have other patients to see."

"Any woman in this hospital would die if I asked them to go out. You have no idea what you're missing, sweetheart," he voiced rather loudly down the hallway.

"Not every woman will be interested in you, Mr. Wolfe!"

I lightly smiled as I shook my head. He was possibly the sexiest man my eyes had ever seen with his six-foot two-inch stature and broad shoulders and biceps that hugged his tight-fitting shirt. His hair was brown and perfectly styled. Short on the sides and longer on top, much like his brothers. A light mustache and five o'clock shadow traced the outline of his masculine jaw. Then there were his eyes. A rich mixture of brown with specs of gold and green throughout. Dreamy and mesmerizing. He was almost perfect. 'Almost' being the keyword. I knew guys like him. All he wanted was sex. There was nothing wrong with that because more times than not, that's all I wanted. I had needs just like every other horny person out in the world, but I didn't like his arrogance, or the fact that he thought every woman he looked at would have sex with him. I moved here for a reason, and one of those reasons wasn't to have sex with some random guy who was the son of one of my patients.

CHAPTER 4

Mason

I walked back into the room with my hands tightly tucked in my pants pockets. I'd admit, she was an incredibly sexy woman. The moment I saw her, I was speechless, which had never happened to me before. She stood about five foot six with long brown hair that was secured in a low ponytail. Her almond-shaped eyes were green with bursts of gold that radiated through them, giving way to her high cheekbones and plump lips that created the perfect face. She was a goddess if I'd ever seen one, and she just flat out rejected me. Needless to say, I was angry about the situation and my brothers knew it the moment I walked through the door.

"What's wrong?" Elijah asked.

"Nothing."

"Where were you?" Nathan raised his brow at me.

"At the nurses' station. Why?"

"I'm going to grab a cup of coffee. If you two want a cup, then come with me," Elijah spoke.

"Sounds good. We'll be right back, Mom," I said as I placed my hand on hers.

"Go ahead. I'm just going to rest my eyes for a bit."

The three of us walked out of the room and headed to the coffee bar in the lobby.

"What's going on?" Elijah asked. "I can tell you're pissed off."

"Yeah, bro. I saw it the minute you came back in the room. What happened?"

"Dr. Sara Davis is what happened. I asked her out for a drink, and she flat out refused."

"Damn." Nathan laughed as he patted me on the back. "Little brother getting rejected by the hot doctor. Ouch. That had to sting."

"Maybe she's married," Elijah chimed in as he ordered us three coffees.

"She's not wearing a ring. I checked."

"Maybe she's a lesbian." Nathan smiled.

"She said she doesn't want to have drinks with me ever and not every woman is going to be interested in me. Do you fucking believe the nerve of her?"

Elijah laughed, and Nathan cocked his head at me.

"Bro, she sounds like Allison when we first met. I can already tell she's a feisty one. Gotta love those feisty girls." He winked.

"Forget about her. Listen, you and Mom went to dinner last night. Was she feeling okay?" I asked Nathan.

"As far as I know. But come to think of it, she barely touched her dinner. She only took a couple bites. When I asked her why she wasn't eating, she said she had a big lunch and wasn't very hungry. But she had an appetite for the manhattans she was kicking back."

"Um, she didn't eat lunch yesterday," Elijah spoke. "I asked her to join me and Aspen and she said she wasn't hungry and didn't want to spoil her appetite for dinner with you." He glanced over at Nathan.

"So she's lying," I said.

"I think we better get in there and find out what's going on with her," Nathan spoke as the three of us headed back to her room.

When we stepped inside, Dr. Davis had just walked in. Damn, what I wouldn't give to hit that just once.

"Your blood sugar is low, Ms. Wolfe. When was the last time you drank alcohol?"

13

"That would be last night. She had quite a few Manhattans at dinner," Nathan said.

"Thank you, son. I appreciate your honesty." My mother narrowed her eye at him.

"Did you eat anything at all yesterday?" Dr. Davis asked. "Ms. Wolfe, I need you to be one hundred percent honest with me. Because if you're not, I will have no choice but to keep you here for a couple of days and do an extensive work up on you. You seem like you're a very busy woman and I'm sure you really don't have the time for that. So, just come clean."

Damn. She was good.

"Fine. I haven't been eating well at all the past couple of weeks, and maybe I have been drinking a little too much alcohol at night."

"Do you want me to ask your boys to step out of the room so we can talk in private?" Dr. Davis asked.

"No. They'll find out, eventually. I ended my relationship with someone I'd been seeing for a long time, and I've been under a great deal of stress."

"Are you serious?" I asked.

"You broke up with Tommy?" Elijah asked.

"Damn, Mom. Why?" Nathan chimed in.

"It's a long story and one I do not want to get into right now. We'll discuss it later."

"Thanks for being honest with me." Sara smiled as she placed her hand on my mother's. "I'm going to order you some lunch. You will eat it all and finish out that IV. So plan on staying here at least a few more hours."

"Fine." My mother rolled her eyes.

"I'll be back to check on you later before you're discharged. It was nice to meet you boys." She nodded to the three of us.

I rolled my eyes and turned away as I stood there with my hands tucked deep inside my pockets.

"Mason, what's wrong?" my mother asked.

"Nothing, Mom."

"Don't lie to me. I know that look."

"He's butt hurt because Dr. Davis turned him down." Nathan smirked.

"Shut the fuck up, douchebag." I smacked him upside the head.

"Ouch. Fuck you, bro."

"That's enough, you two. She's a beautiful woman. She really turned you down, darling?"

"Yeah, Mom. Let's just drop it. I don't care. I found her attractive, asked her to join me for a drink, she said no, and now we'll move on."

"Hey, Mom. You're staying at my house tonight," Nathan spoke, and I shot him a look of disbelief.

"She can stay with me and Aspen," Elijah said.

"No. No. Ruby would love it if you spent the night with us."

"Boys, I know you're concerned, but I'm not staying with any of you. I'll be fine."

"Sorry, Mom, we need to make sure you're okay. You're staying at my house tonight. Just one night. Please, Mom. Don't make us worry about you anymore than we already are. You gave us a scare. Plus, if you aren't with Tommy anymore, you shouldn't be alone."

I knew damn well why Nathan was offering his house as I stood there narrowing my eye at him and at the smirk across his face.

"Plus, Mason will be there if there's an issue. Right, Mason?" He smiled.

"That's actually a good idea, Mom. Mason is medically trained. I would feel better knowing he was there just in case," Elijah spoke.

"Yeah, Mom. It's a good idea," I spoke as I placed my hand on hers.

"Fine. I'll stay with you and Nathan tonight and tonight only."

"Great. I'll go call Allison and let her know," Nathan said as he walked out of the room.

I followed him out and stood there while he talked to Allison. Once he ended the call, I punched him in the arm.

"Bro, enough with the fucking hitting."

"You did that on purpose to get me back for smacking you upside the head." I pointed at him.

"Maybe." He smirked. "But honestly, I'm blown away she broke it

15

off with Tommy and never said a word about it. We need to keep an eye on her."

"I know." I sighed.

"Hey, Dr. Davis." Nathan grinned as she passed by.

"Nathan." She nodded.

"Change your mind yet about that drink?" I asked.

"Nope." She continued walking away.

Nathan chuckled and I when I went to smack him, he grabbed my hand.

"Don't even think about it."

"Will you two grow the fuck up," Elijah said as he walked over to us. "We need to be here for Mom now."

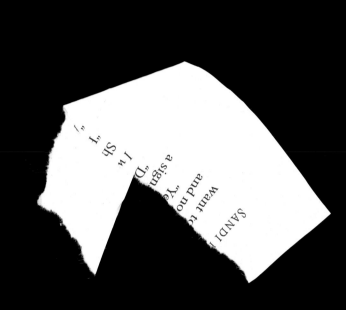

CHAPTER 5

*M*ason

After we brought our mother back to Nathan's and got her settled, Nathan, Elijah and I decided it would be a good idea to go to Rudy's for a couple of drinks. Between last night and today, I needed the whole damn bottle. My mother insisted we went, and Allison and Aspen were both there if any issues arose.

We were sitting at the table kicking back our drinks when I looked over at the door and saw Sara walk in with a few of the girls from the hospital. Her hair was down in sexy waves that flowed over her shoulders. Fuck. I thought she looked sexy in scrubs, but to see her in jeans and a tight-fitting top was too much for my cock to handle.

"Look who just walked in." I gestured.

Nathan and Elijah turned around and then looked back at me.

"I guess she did have plans on getting drinks tonight. Just not with you." Nathan chuckled.

"Shut up, douchebag."

"Go talk to her," Elijah spoke.

"No." I picked up my beer.

"What is wrong with you?" he asked. "This isn't like you. We Wolfe brothers don't give up that easily. Have I taught you nothing? If you want to fuck her, then pursue her. Nathan didn't give up on Allison and now look." He smirked.

"Yeah. No thanks." I put my hand up. "Maybe her rejecting me was a sign."

"Jr. Davis!" Nathan yelled and raised his hand.

I was going to kick his ass.

She turned around and walked over to our table.

"Hello again." She smiled. "How is your mom feeling?"

"A lot better. Thank you," Elijah spoke.

"So, will you be hanging out a lot here too?" I asked with an attitude.

"I don't know. This is my first time here."

"So you *weren't* lying when you said you had plans."

"Actually, I was. They just asked me to come with them about an hour ago." She smirked.

I could feel the anger burning inside me.

"It was nice to see you guys again. I have to get back to the girls."

As soon as she walked away, Elijah and Nathan both stared at me.

"Relax, bro. She's not worth it. No matter how sexy she is," Nathan spoke with a serious tone.

"I better get going," Elijah said as he stood up from his seat. "I need to pick up Aspen and Mila and it's almost Mila's bedtime. You coming?"

"Yeah," Nathan said as he stood up.

"You guys go ahead. I'm going to stop by the fire station on my way back."

"Sure. See you at home, bro," Nathan said.

Walking up to the bar, I asked Hanna for another beer.

"Coming right up, Mason." She smiled. "Hey, I heard about your apartment building. I'm really sorry. But I also heard how you saved that little girl." She smiled.

"Thanks, it's been a little rough."

"Are you staying with your mom?"

"Oh god, no." I laughed. "I'm staying with Nathan until I find another place."

"Oh boy. You two are trouble." She winked. "I'll go get your beer."

"That was you?" Sara walked up behind me.

"What was me?"

"You were the one that saved that little girl last night?"

"Yeah."

"I was the doctor who checked her out when they brought her in. She talked about you, but I didn't make the connection."

Hanna handed me my beer, and I threw some cash on the bar.

"I was just doing my job," I said as I walked away.

"Listen, Mason. I'm sorry, okay? I'm sure you're not used to being told no."

"Actually, I'm not." I turned around and faced her.

"It's just I'm not looking for anything."

"Okay. I'm not either."

"Please." She laughed. "You wanted to buy me a drink hoping we'd have sex by the time the evening ended. I know how guys like you think."

"Guys like me. You don't even know me, Dr. Davis. You're just assuming things in that pretty little head of yours."

"I don't need to know you. I can tell just by looking at you and your body language, Mr. Wolfe."

"Is that so?" I spoke in a harsh tone for I was fed up.

"Yeah, it is so," she shouted. "You're overly confident and you think every woman who looks your way wants you."

I stood there with narrowed eyes in disbelief that I was even listening to what she had to say.

"They usually do." I raised my brow.

She rolled her eyes and shook her head. "Well, I don't. Okay?"

"Fine!" I shouted. "I don't care. Like I said, you don't even know me. You know what? I think you're a little psycho."

"Good. Then stay away from me."

"Trust me. I will."

"Good." She shouted as she turned and walked away.

"Good!" I yelled.

I was furious as I left Rudy's and headed back to Nathan's. Could my life get any worse? I'd had enough of everything. First the fire, then my mother's episode, and now Dr. Sara Davis. Jesus Christ. I just wanted to go home and go to bed.

The moment I walked through the door, I saw Nathan and Allison sitting on the couch in the living room.

"Where's Mom?" I asked.

"She's upstairs sleeping."

"Is she feeling okay?"

"Yeah. She's fine," Allison spoke. "I think she's really depressed over Tommy, though."

"Did she say why she broke up with him?"

"Not yet." Nathan sighed. "She doesn't want to talk about it. Everything okay at the fire station?"

"I didn't make it there. I had a little run in with Dr. Sara Davis after you and Elijah left. That woman is a total psycho."

"Ah, another psycho chick." Allison smiled.

"What happened?" Nathan asked.

"I don't want to talk about it. I'm heading to bed. Good night, you two."

"Night, bro. Sleep tight."

"Night, Mason. Don't give psycho chick another thought."

"I don't plan on it."

CHAPTER 6

*S*ara

I mumbled all the way to the table where the girls sat.
How dare he call me a psycho. He's the psycho one. Oh my God, why
was I letting that man get under my skin.

"Hey. I'm going to go home. It was a long shift and I'm tired."

"Are you sure you can't stay for one more drink?" Corinne asked.

"I'm sure. Thanks for inviting me to come along. Let's do this
again." I gave a soft smile.

"We hang out here a lot, so don't worry. You'll be back. I'll see you
at work," Corinne spoke.

I took a cab back to my Airbnb and started the water for a bath.
After I twisted up my hair, I removed the bubble bar I'd bought from
Lush and crumbled it under the running stream of water. Stepping in
the tub, I let out a deep breath as I slid down into the hot bubbly
water.

I'd been here a week and still didn't have any luck finding an
apartment I liked or wanted to call home. I needed to find something
ASAP before my contract with the owners of the Airbnb was up
because they already had it rented out to someone else. I honestly
didn't think I'd have this much trouble finding a place. It had to be the

perfect apartment for I wasn't planning on moving again until I could afford a townhome. Before I moved to New York permanently, I had been looking at apartments and came to the city on my days off from the hospital to tour them. Nothing grabbed my attention except one, and unfortunately, there was a waiting list. I knew the moment I stepped inside; it was where I belonged. It felt right and very cozy. Even though the rent was higher than I wanted to pay, the best part was, every apartment in the building came fully furnished. All I had to do was move in. The thought made me happy because I honestly didn't have time to furniture shop. But that was just a dream because there was no way I'd be getting a call anytime soon that one was available.

Grabbing my phone, I scrolled through the listing of apartments in the city. I needed to stay in the area, so it limited my options. That was another perk of the apartment I fell in love with. It was the perfect location.

After drying off and getting into my pajamas, I poured a glass of wine and set it on the nightstand while I climbed in bed. With my glass in one hand and my phone in the other, I scrolled through as many listings as I could and saved a few that looked decent so I could call tomorrow and see if I could take a tour since I had the day off.

❧

I sighed as I walked out of the last apartment I toured. Out of the four buildings I looked at, only one apartment was okay. The location was convenient; the price was right, but it was smaller than what I wanted, and it didn't give off the homey vibe I'd been looking for. At this point, I really had no choice. I had one more apartment to tour, but I'd already had a feeling it wouldn't work out for me. As I was heading there, my phone rang with an unfamiliar number.

"Hello."

"Hi, is this Sara Davis?" the woman on the other end asked.

"Yes."

"Hi Miss Davis, this is Renee from Altman Building Properties. You asked to be put on our waiting list when an apartment became available."

My heart started racing.

"Yes. Do you have one?"

"We do. It's a twelve hundred square foot two-bedroom, two bath which will be available and ready to move in on Friday. It's been fully refurnished with brand new furniture throughout, and the rent is ten thousand a month. I know you were interested in a one bedroom, but honestly, there won't be one available within the next few months. So, I'm calling to see if you're interested in the two bedroom we have."

Shit. Ten thousand a month was way more than I wanted to pay, but I hadn't stopped thinking about it since I toured the model apartment a few weeks ago. It was bigger and who didn't need more space.

"I'll take it," I spoke.

"Excellent. When would you be available to sign the lease?"

"I can come now if that's okay."

"That would be perfect. I'll see you soon."

Excitement soared through me as I placed my phone in my purse and took a cab to my new apartment.

CHAPTER 7

Mason

"Good morning." I smiled as I walked into the kitchen.

"Morning, bro. How did you sleep?" Nathan asked.

"Good."

He poured me a cup of coffee and handed it to me.

"Where's Mom?"

"She and Allison already left for the office."

"Should she be going to work today?"

"She said she's fine, and she ate some breakfast before they left. It's not like I could stop her. She's mom, and she's stubborn."

"True."

"Good morning, Uncle Mason." Ruby grinned as she gave me a hug.

"Morning, peanut."

"I'm ready for school, Dad."

"Okay. Let's go. Be ready when I get back and we'll go for a run." Nathan pointed at me.

"Sounds good, bro. I need to go shopping today for some clothes. I go back to the station tomorrow."

"Okay. I'll go with you. I'm not doing anything today, but we have to be back for Ruby."

Ruby and Nathan left, and I made myself some scrambled eggs. As I was sitting at the table looking at my phone, it rang with an unfamiliar number.

"Hello."

"Hi, I'm looking for Mason Wolfe."

"This is he."

"Mr. Wolfe, this is Victoria from Altman Building Properties. I'm calling to inform you that a twelve hundred square foot two-bedroom, two bath apartment is available if you're still interested."

"Victoria, sweetheart, you just made my day. I am definitely interested. When will it be ready for move in?"

"Friday. I'm actually working from home today and I have the lease agreement with me. I can come by your place to have you sign it if that's okay."

"Perfect." I rattled off the address.

"All I'll need is a ten-thousand-dollar deposit, and the apartment is yours. I can take a check or credit card."

"Not a problem."

"Great. I can swing by your place in about an hour. Will that work?"

"I'll be here. Thank you."

I ended the call with a smile on my face. I'd been on the waiting list for that building for six months. If my previous building hadn't burnt down, my lease would have been up in a couple of months and I was looking to move. Altman Building Properties was a newer and high demand building that was built three years ago.

"Why aren't you ready?" Nathan asked as he stepped into the kitchen and found me still sitting at the table.

"Change of plans. I got a call from Victoria from Altman Building Properties. A two-bedroom apartment is available and she's bringing the lease over for me to sign in about an hour."

"Wow. Talk about perfect timing. You were on a waiting list, weren't you?"

"Yeah for about six months."

"I don't know why you just don't buy a townhouse, bro."

"Why? I'm a bachelor, and a townhouse is way too much room for one person. Before you met Allison and Ruby, you would never have bought this place."

"I guess you're right. Why is Victoria coming here? I didn't know leasing agents made house calls."

"She said she's working from home today. I'm going to hop in the shower. Can I borrow a shirt?"

"Yeah. I'll go grab you one. After you sign your lease, we'll head to the stores. I was thinking maybe we should stop at the law firm and check on Mom."

"Good idea."

After I showered and dressed, I ran downstairs to wait for Victoria. The shirt Nathan gave me was a little tight, especially around my arms.

"Bro, you really need to work out your biceps more," I spoke as I walked downstairs. "This shirt barely fits because I'm so much bigger than you." I smirked.

"Shut the fuck up. I'll out press you next time we go to the gym."

"You wish." I playfully punched him in the chest.

The doorbell rang, and I told Nathan I got it. When I opened the door, there was a woman standing there holding a baby and a briefcase.

"Mr. Wolfe? Sorry about this. My babysitter cancelled at the last minute. Hence the reason I'm working from home today."

"Not a problem. Come on in and we'll go into the kitchen. Can I get you a cup of coffee?"

"No thanks. I'm good."

"Victoria, this is my brother Nathan."

"Nice to meet you. I'd shake your hand, but they're a little full right now."

As soon as she took a seat at the table, the baby started to cry. She bounced him on her knee as she struggled with her briefcase. "There's no reason for him to be crying. He's been fed and changed. I'm so sorry."

"It's okay, Victoria. You can give the baby to Nathan while we do this. For some reason, babies love him." I furrowed my brows.

"Oh my gosh, do you mind?" she asked him.

"Not at all. Come here, little guy," Nathan spoke as he took the crying baby from her arms.

He looked at Nathan and instantly stopped crying.

"See. I told you." I smiled. "How old is he?"

"Seven months," she replied as she took out the lease papers from her briefcase.

I signed the lease, handed her my credit card, and it was a done deal. In a few days, I'd be moving into my new apartment and start living my bachelor life once again.

CHAPTER 8

*S*ara

I packed up my things and took one last look around the Airbnb to make sure I wasn't leaving anything behind. Finally, I was moving into a place I could call my own. When I walked into the building, Vinnie, the doorman greeted me. He tipped his hat with a smile and welcomed me to the building. It had already felt like home. Taking the elevator up to the nineteenth floor, I found apartment 19A and was caught off guard when I discovered the door wasn't locked. Stepping inside, I rolled my two large suitcases in and shut the door.

"I thought you weren't—What the hell?" Mason emerged from the hallway and stopped dead in his tracks.

"Mason? What is going on? Why are you in my apartment?"

"I was just going to ask you the same thing, Sara. Why are there two suitcases sitting there?"

My heart pounded out of my chest. What the fuck was going on?

"Explain to me right now why you're standing in my apartment!" I loudly voiced.

"Your apartment? This is my apartment!"

"No. No, it's not. I have my lease right here!" I pulled the paper from my purse.

"So do I!" He walked over to the island in the kitchen and held it up.

My mind was confused, and I couldn't comprehend what was happening. I was trained for chaos, but I couldn't wrap my head around what the hell was going on. Setting down my purse, I placed my hands on each side of my head and paced around the room.

"I can't believe this," I spoke in a panic.

"I'll call the leasing office and find out what the hell is going on," he spoke as he pulled his phone from his pocket. "Victoria said she'll be up in a few minutes."

"Who's Victoria?"

"The leasing agent. You didn't deal with her?"

"No. I dealt with Renee."

There was a knock on the door and Victoria stepped inside.

"I—I can't even explain what happened here with your leases," she spoke.

"Well, you better start because this is a tremendous problem," Mason spoke.

"Renee is new and handled things on her own when she shouldn't have."

"Okay. So now what?" I asked her.

"Well, one of you will have to vacate the apartment. It's up to you who goes. I looked over both your leases and they were signed at the same exact time, so it's no longer a matter of who signed first."

"You're kidding me," Mason spoke.

"I wish I was Mr. Wolfe. I cannot apologize enough for this. I can assure you this will never happen again."

"Your assurances don't help us in this situation, Victoria. How the hell can you let two different people sign two leases for the same apartment? I'm calling my brother, Elijah." He pulled out his phone as I sat there in tears on the couch.

"Why?" I asked.

"Because he and my mother are lawyers and they'll get this matter cleared up quickly. I have been on that waiting list for six months. Surely that says something."

"Yeah, well, I signed a lease too!" I stood up in anger.

"We both did. So I'll call Elijah and we'll get this sorted out. There isn't another apartment available?" he asked Victoria.

"No. I wish to god there was, and unfortunately, nobody has plans on moving out anytime soon. I'm so sorry about this. I'll need your decision by tomorrow. If you both work it out and stay, I will draw up another lease for you with both your names on it for you to sign."

"And what if you were in my shoes?" I snapped at her. "Would you live with a total stranger? You messed this up." I pointed my finger at her. "And I expect you to fix it! You know what, call your brother, Mason. I think a good lawsuit is in order here."

"I'm sorry you feel that way. I'll talk to you both tomorrow."

She walked out of the apartment and I let out a scream.

"Seriously, just calm down," Mason spoke.

"NO! I won't calm down, and I'm not leaving my apartment!" I shouted as I stood there with my arms folded, staring at him.

"Well, I'm not leaving either." He brought his phone up to his ear. "Elijah, I have a problem and I need your advice ASAP. No, I'm not being sued for sexual harassment." He rolled his eyes. "It's an issue with my lease. Okay. I'll be there in a few. Make sure you have your lease and let's go," he said as he grabbed his key from the counter and headed towards the door.

We both climbed into the back of a cab and I didn't say a word as I stared out the window. I couldn't believe this was happening and with him of all people. What were the odds of this happening? One in a trillion? The ride to his brother's law firm was silent. He didn't speak a word, and neither did I. We entered the building and took the elevator up to the 37th floor. When we stepped out, a young blonde woman sitting behind a mahogany desk flirtatiously greeted Mason.

"Hey, Mason." Her teeth grazed her bottom lip.

"Good morning." He smiled at her as we walked by. "Hey, Marie. Is he in there?"

"Hi, Mason. He said he'll be right back and to have a seat. Who's this pretty lady with you?" She grinned.

"Dr. Sara Davis. Sara, this is Elijah's secretary, Marie."

"It's nice to meet you, Marie." I extended my hand.

"Nice to meet you too, Dr."

"Mason?" Allison walked over. "What are you doing here?"

"Hey, Allison. I'm having some trouble with my new lease and I need Elijah's help."

"Let's go in his office. He's finishing up with a client. Hi, I'm Allison." She extended her hand.

"Hi, I'm Sara Davis."

"As in Dr. Davis, who treated your mother?" She glanced at Mason with a smile.

"Yes. Allison is Nathan's fiancée," he spoke to me.

"You're here," Elijah spoke as he walked in and stopped dead in his tracks when he saw Sara standing there.

CHAPTER 9

*M*ason
"Dr. Davis. It's nice to see you again." Elijah extended his hand. "What is going on here?" he asked as he took a seat behind his desk and Allison walked out, shutting the door behind her.

"The leasing agent at my apartment building leased the same apartment to both of us." We both handed our leases to him.

"To both of you?" He pointed at each of us as he let out a chuckle.

"This isn't funny, Elijah."

"Oh, but it is, little brother."

He looked over the identical leases and let out a sigh.

"How did this happen?" he asked.

"One agent called me, and another called Sara without the two of them knowing they were renting the same apartment."

"It is illegal to have two active leases for the same property. What did the leasing agent tell you?"

"She said one of us has to move out and we have until tomorrow to let her know who it'll be. The problem is neither one of us will leave." I shot Sara a look. "So I need you to advise me on how to make her leave."

"Excuse me!" she snapped. "It isn't my fault they screwed up."

"And it's not mine either!"

"Okay. Let's calm down. The only thing I can tell you is one of you has to move out." He closely looked at the lease again. "How is it possible that the two of you signed these leases at the same exact time? Didn't you see each other in the leasing office?"

"I didn't go to the leasing office. Victoria, the leasing agent, came to Nathan's, and I signed it there. She was working from home that day."

"Ah, I see." He let out a sigh.

"I'm sorry to—" My mother walked into the office and immediately came to a halt when she saw us sitting there. "Dr. Davis?"

"Hello, Ms. Wolfe. How are you feeling?"

"Please, call me Caitlin. I'm feeling much better. Thank you. Why are the two of you here? And more importantly, why are you here together?"

"Apparently Mason's new apartment building leased the same apartment to Sara," Elijah spoke as he held up both leases.

"What? So they're collecting rent from both of you? That is highly illegal."

"The landlord is giving them until tomorrow to decide on who will leave the apartment."

"I see. Who signed the lease first?" she asked.

"They both signed it at the same exact time," Elijah replied.

"Oh. Wow. That's weird." She cocked her head at us.

"Well, you two work it out. Elijah, I need you to sign these documents by this afternoon. It was good to see you again, Dr. Davis." She smiled at her. "I'll talk to you later, Mason."

"Sure thing, Mom." I sighed. "Okay so what are we supposed to do?" I asked my brother.

"One of you has to decide who moves out. If either of you decides to sue the landlord, it can be arranged. We'd go for punitive damages and emotional distress. We'd win, but it would take some time. My advice to you is that you go somewhere quiet and talk it out. You're both adults and there are a million apartments in New York to choose from. Mason, you're a captain for the New York Fire Department and Sara, you're a doctor. You're both professionals and you need to discuss this situation as such. I'm sorry this happened, and I know it isn't fair, but there's nothing we can do about it. The leasing office screwed up. I can't force them to make another apartment available."

"Thanks, bro," I said as I stood from my chair.

"Thanks, Elijah. I appreciate your advice," Sara spoke.

"You're welcome. I'm here anytime you need me. Let me know what you decide and if either one of you want to proceed with a lawsuit."

We walked out of the building and stood at the curb while I grabbed us a cab. We sat there in silence for a few moments until I couldn't take it anymore.

"Sara, we have to talk about this at some point."

"There's nothing to talk about. I'm not leaving."

I sighed as I turned my head and looked out the window. It was going to be a long day.

When we arrived back to the apartment, we both took out our keys, but mine made it first into the lock. I opened the door and motioned for her to go in first.

"Like Elijah said, we're both adults and we need to have an adult conversation about this", I spoke as she sat down on the couch. "Didn't you already have an apartment?"

"Didn't you?" she spoke in a harsh tone.

"No. My apartment building burnt down. That night Olivia was brought to the ER, she lived down the hall from me. I lost everything that night in the fire. Pretty much my entire life was reduced to ashes."

"Oh. I'm sorry about that." She looked up at me. "But you have your family you can stay with. I have nobody. I just moved here, and I have nowhere else to go except some damn hotel for god knows how long."

"I'm not living with my family. I'm staying here, in MY apartment I've waited for, for the last six months. I'm sorry they screwed you, but that's not my problem."

34

"I know exactly what this is and why you're doing this."

"Enlighten me, please."

"You're using this as revenge against me because I wouldn't go out with you."

"HA!" I laughed. "Is that what you really think? I don't do revenge, Sara. I'm not leaving because this place is rightfully mine."

CHAPTER 10

*S*ara

"Rightfully yours?" I stood up. "Who the hell do you think you are? Oh wait. That's right. The great Captain Mason Wolfe who saves children from burning buildings."

"Wow." He stood there with a narrowed eye. "I am so happy I dodged that bullet."

"What bullet?"

"You. I'm happy you turned me down for a drink. Because in all honesty, I don't even want to get to know a person like you. For a doctor, you sure as hell aren't caring or compassionate."

Ouch.

I wanted to scream at him, lash out, but I didn't. He had no idea what I was going through. I could feel the sting in my eyes as the tears came to the surface. I turned away from him and stared out the window because I couldn't let him see me cry. He was wrong about me. I was caring and compassionate. I was just angry. Angry about this whole mess I was in. I didn't want to move to New York, but I didn't have a choice. I was doing the right thing and somehow, it seemed to bite me in the ass.

"You're just going to stand there and not say anything?"

"I'm sorry for what I said. The apartment is yours," I spoke without turning to face him.

Wiping the tear that fell down my cheek, I walked over to where my suitcases sat, grabbed them and my purse and headed towards the door.

"Are you crying?" he asked.

"No." I lied as I sniffled.

I felt his hand lightly grab my arm as he turned me around.

"You are crying. Sara—"

"Don't, Mason. Enjoy your new place."

He let go of my arm as I struggled to open the door.

"Tell Victoria that I left and to please refund me my deposit. I have to go call the movers and have them deliver my things somewhere else," I walked out.

"Sara, wait." I heard his voice as I began walking down the hallway. "Where are you going to go?"

"I'll find somewhere."

"For fuck's sake. Get back inside."

I pushed the button to the elevator and prayed the doors would open quickly, but they didn't. Mason walked over to me and grabbed one of my suitcases from my hand.

"What the hell are you doing?"

"Taking your suitcase back inside. At least stay the night."

"No, Mason. Give me back my suitcase."

He walked inside the apartment with it and shut the door. I sighed as I hurried back to the apartment and opened the door.

"Wolfe, give me back my suitcase!"

"I'm not letting you walk out of here without a plan. It's not happening. Not tonight. Stay the night and make a plan."

"I can do that from a hotel room."

"I wouldn't feel right. It's not your fault this happened."

"Damn right it's not." I stood there with my arms folded.

"Just take the rest of today and tonight to make a plan."

"Fine. I'll stay, but don't expect me to be social. I'll just go to one of

37

the bedrooms and decide what I'm going to do. Which bedroom did you already claim?" I asked.

"The one over here. Both rooms are the same size, so don't accuse me of taking the bigger one."

"I really don't care if you did. It's not my apartment anymore."

I took both my suitcases, went into the bedroom and shut the door. Throwing myself on the queen-size bed, I looked up at the ceiling, letting the tears roll back into my eyes. My phone rang, and when I pulled it out, I saw Karen was calling.

"Hello."

"Sara, it's Karen. I thought you should know that your mother is having a good day, and she's asking for you."

"She is?"

"Yes. I thought maybe you'd want to come see her."

"Of course, I'll be right there."

I grabbed my purse and flew through the apartment.

"Where are you going?" Mason asked.

"Out. I'll be back in a while."

Even though my mother was in a state of reality for a short while, it was good to be able to hold a conversation with her, even if it was only for a few hours. Days like these were far and few between anymore. She recognized me the moment I stepped into her room and she gave me a hug. We went for a walk outside and took in the beauty mother nature had to offer. I treasured every second I was with her until she slipped away, back into the cracks that filled her mind and into the fog that consumed her well-being.

After I left Easton Gardens, I realized I hadn't eaten all day. I was starving, so I stopped and picked up a pizza. I wanted to ask Mason what he liked, but I didn't have his number. When I walked through the door, I set the pizza on the island and Mason came from his room.

"Hey," he spoke.

"Hey. I brought a pizza home. Well, to your home. Have a piece. There's plenty there."

"Are you sure?"

"Yeah, of course. Do you have any plates?"

"Yeah. They came with the apartment. Four of everything, including the silverware," he said as he reached up into the cabinet.

After he handed me my plate, I put two slices of pizza on it and took it over to the table.

"How about a bottle of beer to go with your pizza?" he asked.

"Sure."

He handed me my beer and took the seat across from me. We sat there in awkward silence for a few moments while we ate.

"Is everything okay?" Mason asked.

"Yeah. Why?" I picked up my beer.

"I don't know. It's just the way you ran out of here. Like there was an emergency or something."

Did I tell him about my mom? Dare I open that door? It didn't matter because after tonight, I probably wouldn't see him again. Maybe only in passing at the hospital or at the bar.

"I went to see my mom."

"Your mom lives here?" he asked with a confused look on his face.

"Yes. She lives over at Easton Gardens."

"The assisted living home for people with Alzheimer's?"

"Yeah. You know it?"

"Yeah. We get called there a lot. I'm sorry. I didn't know."

"Thanks. She was having a good day today and was asking for me, so Karen called to let me know. It isn't often she has days like that, so I take every opportunity I can get."

"How long has she had Alzheimer's?"

"It started four years ago and just this past year it got really bad. Easton Gardens is one of the best in the country. That's why I brought her here."

"I know it is, and it's only a couple blocks away. May I ask how old she is?"

"She's fifty-nine."

"Damn. She's still young."

Suddenly, there was a knock at the door. Mason got up and when he opened it, Nathan stepped inside.

CHAPTER 11

*M*ason

"Nathan, when did you get back?"

"A while ago. Allison and Ruby are with Aspen and Mila, so I came by to check out your new place. Is that Dr. Davis?" he whispered with a smile as he glanced over my shoulder. "So you did manage to score with her."

"God no. It's been a clusterfuck of a day and you won't believe it. Come on in."

"Dr. Davis, it's nice to see you again."

"Hi, Nathan. You can call me Sara."

"So, what's going on here?" he asked. "By the way, great place."

"I'll let you tell him the story," Sara said as she got up and placed her plate in the dishwasher. "I'll go make a plan. It was nice to see you, Nathan."

Nathan gave her a smile and then turned to me.

"What the fuck is going on? What did I miss? This is why I hate being gone for more than a day."

I sighed as I sat down.

"Go grab a beer and a slice of pizza and prepare yourself."

"So, what is doctor hottie doing here?" he asked as he brought his plate back to the table.

"The landlord inadvertently leased the apartment to both her and me. One of us has until tomorrow morning to let them know who's moving out."

"You can't be serious, bro." His brow arched.

"I'm dead serious. We talked to Elijah about it. There isn't anything we can do."

"So I take it you kicked her to the curb?"

"I did. She'll be gone in the morning."

"Where will she go?"

"I don't know. I told her she could stay tonight so she could make a plan."

"And she just accepted that?"

"Hell no. There was a lot of arguing, yelling and tears on her part."

"I'm sure there was. She doesn't seem like the type that would give up without a fight."

"She's not. But ultimately, she did, and I'm not sure why."

"You know, bro, if you're having second thoughts you can stay with me and Allison until you find another place."

"Nah. This apartment is rightfully mine. I've been on the waiting list for six months, and I am not giving it up because the landlord fucked up. Welcome to my new bachelor pad, bro." I grinned.

"I love it, and I know there will be many sexually fulfilled nights here." He tipped his bottle to mine.

His phone dinged and when he pulled it out of his pocket and read Allison's text, he immediately got up from his seat.

"Gotta go. Allison and Ruby are home."

"Do you always jump when she texts you?"

"Of course. I love her and I missed them."

"You've only been gone a couple of days."

"Doesn't matter. Even a few hours without them is enough to drive me crazy."

I rolled my eyes as I got up from my seat and gave him a bro hug.

"I'll talk to you later. Love the place, bro," he said as he walked out the door.

&

S ara
The morning sun beamed through the blinds as I opened my eyes and wiped the sleep from them. Climbing out of bed, I quickly made it and then went into the bathroom to wash my face and brush my teeth. After pulling my hair back in a ponytail, I got dressed and pulled my suitcases behind me as I left my room. The door opened and Mason walked in carrying a cup holder in one hand and a white box in the other.

"Good morning," he spoke.

"Good morning."

"I brought us some coffee and donuts. I figured you'd need some fuel before you leave."

"Thanks, Mason," I said as I took one of the cups from the holder.

"Did you make a plan last night?" he asked as he grabbed a donut from the box.

"Yeah. I booked a room at the Hilton, and I made an appointment to tour an apartment I looked at before. I want to see it again before I make a final decision."

"Listen, Sara," he spoke as he leaned up against the counter. "I think you should just stay here."

"Really? You'd move out and let me have it?"

"No. We can be roommates."

My heart leapt into my throat.

"I don't think that's a good idea. We don't get along very well."

"I'm usually gone three nights a week and with your schedule, I'm sure you're not home much either. So, we'd barely see each other."

"I don't like to share," I said as I took a bite of my glazed donut.

"Trust me. I don't either. I'm not taking this lightly. You need to understand how hard this is for me to even offer. I don't do roommates, and I like my personal space."

"I like my personal space, and I don't do roommates either. Not even in college or med school. I've always been on my own. Why the sudden change of heart?" My eye steadily narrowed at him.

"Because I'm not willing to move out and you don't want to move, so I think as adults we can compromise."

"You're serious, aren't you?"

"Yeah, I am. We can split the bills. It'll be cheaper for both of us, and I'm willing to try if you are."

"We'd have to come up with a list of rules."

"Definitely." He smiled.

I sat there and stared at him while I sipped my coffee. What was he up to?

"You're not offering because you think I'll have sex with you, are you?"

"No. That ship already sailed. If you reject me once, I move on and I don't look back. The truth is, I'm sure you wanted this place because it's close to the hospital and to your mom. You need to be close to her in case of an emergency or something."

"Thanks, Mason. I appreciate it, but a lot of things were said yesterday between us."

"I know, and I'm willing to put that behind me and move forward. We don't have to be friends, Sara. We can just be two people who share an apartment that barely see each other. You stay out of my way, and I'll stay out of yours."

"Can I at least have your phone number in case there's an emergency?" I asked.

"Yes, and I'll need yours. You in?"

I hesitated for a moment and took in a deep breath.

"I'm in. Thank you." I gave him a soft smile.

"Okay. Let's go to the office and tell Victoria to draw up a new lease. But first, let's take these suitcases back to your room," he said as he grabbed them.

Was this a good idea? Probably not. As much as he irritated me, it was nice of him to offer that we share the apartment. I could do this.

Like he said, he'd be gone three nights a week and with my crazy work schedule, we'd probably never see each other much.

After we signed the new lease, we went back up to the apartment, sat at the table and made a list of rules each of us were to follow.

1. No touching food that doesn't belong to you.
2. Take turns cleaning the apartment and stay on top of the cleaning schedule.
3. Do your own shopping.
4. Bills will be divided equally and paid on time.
5. No borrowing of personal things without asking.
6. Be respectful of personal space.
7. Get party permission before throwing the party.
8. No dishes piling in the sink.
9. Be respectful when having overnight guests. Keep noise level to a minimum.
10. Respect each other's privacy.

"Can you think of anything else?"

"I think that should do it," I spoke.

There was a knock at the door, and I immediately jumped up.

"That must be the movers with my things."

As soon as they stepped inside, I directed them to take all my boxes to the bedroom while I canceled my reservation at the Hilton.

CHAPTER 12

*M*ason

The thing I dreaded the most was having to tell my family what I'd done. I would never hear the end of it. The truth was, Sara was going through some shit I didn't know about and I didn't want to add the stress of her being homeless to it. As long as we followed the rules we set in place, and I stopped thinking about fucking her every which possible, we'd be fine.

I walked into my mother's house for family dinner, and I braced myself for the teasing and comments I was about to receive once I told them about Sara.

"Hey," I spoke as I walked into the kitchen with my hands tucked into my pants pockets.

"Hello, darling." My mother smiled as she walked over and kissed my cheek.

"Well?" Elijah spoke. "I've been waiting to hear from you all day."

"Yeah, bro, me too. I was going to call you when I didn't hear anything, but I figured you had your hands full with Sara."

I took in a deep breath.

"I told her she could stay. She's officially my roommate now."

"You what!" Nathan laughed and Elijah didn't say a word.

"Are you sure you know what you're doing?" my mother asked.

"How did she talk you into that?" Elijah asked.

"She didn't. I offered. Her mother is a resident over at Easton Gardens."

"The assisted living home for patients with Alzheimer's?" my mother asked.

"Yes. The primary reason she wanted the apartment was because it's close. She's dealing with a lot. She's in a new city, her mother is in stage four Alzheimer's and she was homeless thanks to the landlord fucking up. What the hell was I supposed to do?"

My mother walked over and placed her hand on my cheek.

"I am so proud of you. You did the right thing. You should have brought her to dinner."

I gave her a small smile as Nathan hooked his arm around me.

"Does this mean she'll let you in her bed now?"

"No, and I'm not even thinking about that anymore. We wrote out a list of rules."

"Good idea," Elijah said.

"Rules? Who the hell are you, and what have you done with my brother?" Nathan spoke as he put me in a headlock.

"Knock it off, bro. I'm serious. This wasn't an easy decision."

"Do you think she told you about her mother for sympathy knowing you'd possibly let her move in?" Elijah asked me.

"Nah. She wouldn't have mentioned it if I didn't ask her where she went that night."

"All I know is I'm going to sit back and watch this shitshow unfold." Nathan grinned, and I punched him.

❧

One Week Later

I'd just gotten home from the fire station and when I walked through the door, I saw Sara sitting on the couch with her laptop.

46

"Hey," She glanced over my way.

"Hi." I walked over to the couch and sat down next to her.

"You smell like a fire." She smiled.

"That's because I was just in one. I didn't shower at the station. My shift was over, and I just came home. I thought you worked tonight."

"I was, but one of the other doctors needed tomorrow off so he asked if I could switch with him and work his shift tomorrow."

I stared at her as I cocked my head.

"What?" She laughed.

"I think this is the most conversation we've had since we moved in together."

"I guess so." The corners of her mouth curved upward. "We really haven't seen each other."

"I'm going to take a shower." I stood up. "Did you eat dinner yet?"

"No. I was thinking about ordering some Chinese food."

"That sounds like an excellent idea." I pointed my finger at her. "Order me a quart of sweet and sour chicken, a pint of shrimp fried rice and an egg roll." Reaching into my pants pocket, I took out my wallet and handed her my credit card. "My treat tonight. Order anything you want. You can buy next time."

"If you insist." She grinned as she took the card from my hand.

When I finished showering, I threw on a pair of sweatpants and a t-shirt and went into the kitchen and grabbed a beer from the refrigerator.

"Did you order it yet?" I shouted through the apartment.

"Yes. It'll be here soon." I heard her voice coming from her bedroom.

CHAPTER 13

*S*ara

I changed into a pair of cotton shorts, a tank top, and threw my hair up in a high ponytail when I heard a knock at the door.

"I got it," I spoke as I walked past him sitting on the couch.

I took the bag over to the table while Mason grabbed some plates from the cabinet.

"Do you want a beer?" he asked.

"Sure," I said as I took out the cartons of food.

"What did you order?" Mason asked as he took the cap off the bottle and set it down by my plate.

"Honey Chicken and an egg roll."

"Sounds good."

He took his seat across from me and began plating his food.

"You never did tell me where you're from," he spoke.

"Does it matter?" I smirked.

"Kind of. Since we're roommates, I should know a little about you. What if you're a psycho killer?" He gave me a sexy wink.

"True, and the same goes for you. I'm from New Haven, Connecticut."

"Great place. I used to go visit some friends up at Yale."

"Really?" I cocked my head at him. "I went to Yale."

"Wow. Look at you, miss fancy pants. I had no idea I was sharing a space with a Yale graduate." A smirk crossed his lips.

"Maybe we saw each other up there at some point and just don't remember," I said as I took a bite of my egg roll.

"Doubt it. I would definitely remember someone as beautiful as you."

My heart started to race as I nearly choked on my egg roll.

"Okay. So now that I know you went to Yale, tell me why you decided to become a doctor."

"My mom was a doctor, and I spent a lot of time hanging around the ER. Plus, I like to help people. "What about you? Why a firefighter?"

"I do it for the adrenaline rush." He grinned as he shoved a piece of chicken in his mouth.

"I find it hard to believe that's the only reason."

"You're right. I've always loved fires. I would intentionally start them just so I could put them out."

"What?" I laughed. "What are you, some kind of pyromaniac?"

He let out a chuckle. "My mom thought I was. But all kidding aside, they were just tiny containable fires in the backyard. One night, when I was thirteen, I was walking home from a friend's house and the townhome down the block was on fire. The fire department wasn't there yet and when I stared at it, I saw Mr. Fields in the window upstairs screaming for help. I somehow knew if he stayed in there any longer, he would die. So, I ran inside, ran up the stairs and got him out. The adrenaline that rushed through me that night was incredible, but so was saving Mr. Fields. That fire changed my life. I used to believe it was all about the fires, but it wasn't. It's about human life and the ability to save them. It's about sacrifice and serving my community."

"You know that puts you up on a hero pedestal." I smiled.

"Same goes for you." The corners of his mouth curved upward. "You save people's lives every day."

"It's different for me. I don't put my life on the line saving them like you do."

"It's no different, Sara. A life is a life, no matter how we save them."

Our eyes locked onto each other's and the air around me felt constricted. I gave him a small smile as I grabbed my beer bottle and tipped it to my lips.

"What kind of medicine did your mom practice?"

"She was a cardiothoracic surgeon. In fact, she was one of the best in the country. That was before—" I looked down at my plate.

"Before the Alzheimer's set in?" he asked.

"Yeah. She was a brilliant surgeon and someone I looked up to my whole life."

"What about your father? You never mentioned him."

"Nor have you mentioned yours?" I smirked.

"I don't talk about him." He looked away from me.

"And I don't talk about my father either. So, let's just end it on that note." I held up my beer bottle to him.

"Sounds good to me." He tipped his bottle to mine.

"Your mom seems like a really cool person." I smiled. "I like her."

He sighed as he lightly shook his head.

"She's a handful and you'll see what I'm talking about because she'll be popping in every so often to check on me and butt into my life. Especially since we're living together."

I let out a laugh.

"Can I give you a piece of advice?"

"Sure. Lay it on me," he spoke.

"Treasure every moment you have with her. Even when she butts into your life and you absolutely hate it. Never take the time spent with her for granted, because one day, you won't have those moments anymore."

I watched as he inhaled a sharp breath before bringing the bottle up to his lips.

"I'm really sorry about your mom."

"Thanks. So am I." I pushed my plate away. "It's hard, you know. Dealing with it all. Anyway, I owe you an apology, Mr. Mason Wolfe."

"For what?"

"For the things I said to you when we first met. I assumed things about you I shouldn't have and for that, I'm sorry."

"Nah, Sara. You don't need to apologize. I know I came on a little strong. I should have dialed it back. And for that, I'm the one who's sorry."

"I appreciate that, Mason." I gave him a small smile.

He held up his beer bottle.

"To the start of a new friendship." He grinned.

"To the start of a new friendship." I tipped my bottle to his as I stared into his eyes.

CHAPTER 14

$\mathcal{M}$ason

She was beautiful, and the need to take her to my bed intensified. But we were roommates, and we had rules. As much as I wanted to break those rules, I shouldn't. I didn't want to jeopardize our new friendship. How could I sleep with her when I'd have to see her all the time? That wasn't how it worked with me. One time, maybe two, and then I'd never see them again. It was best that way and getting attached wasn't an option. Regardless of how both my brothers let their guard down and I saw how happy they were, I was still adamant about where I stood as far as relationships were concerned.

Sara was broken, and for the first time tonight, I saw just how broken she was. Besides having to deal with her mother's illness, she was battling the same demons about her father that I was about mine. I could sense it in her voice when she said she didn't talk about him.

"So, since we're celebrating our newfound friendship, I have one more question for you," I said as I got up and grabbed a couple more beers from the fridge.

"Sure. Ask away."

"Did you leave someone behind in Connecticut?" I set her beer down in front of her and took my seat.

She narrowed her eye at me for a moment as she brought the bottle up to her lips.

"What? It's a fair question coming from a friend and roommate." I smirked.

"The answer to your question is no. I don't trust men. No offense."

"None taken." I put my hand up.

She stared out the window for a moment as she ran her hand up and down the beer bottle. I could feel my cock twitching as I watched her.

"I've devoted my life to my medical career and education. Although, I did let my guard down once and dated a guy for almost a year, but then he confirmed why I didn't trust men."

"He cheated on you?"

"He sure did. Not once, not twice, but three different times with three different women. I'd only found out because one of the women, whom I was friends with, told me because she felt bad."

"Wow. What a douchebag. And your father? You said he was the reason you don't trust men."

"I don't talk about him. Remember?"

"Right. Sorry."

My phone rang, and Allison was calling.

"Hey, Allison."

"Mason, I'm with your mom at her house and she's not feeling well again. I just made her go lie down. I thought you should know. I tried to call Elijah, but he didn't answer. And Nathan is still at work."

"I'm on my way. Make sure she stays in bed."

"What's wrong?" Sara asked.

"My mother isn't feeling well again. Allison is with her now. I'm heading over there."

"Let me grab my bag and I'll go with you. If that's okay?"

"Sure. I'd appreciate that."

We both got up from our seats and headed over to the townhouse.

Opening the door, we stepped inside where Allison greeted us in the foyer.

"What happened?" I asked.

"We were going over the invitations for the wedding and she got really dizzy and said she felt like she was going to pass out. I gave her some orange juice and made her get in bed."

"Lead the way to the bedroom so I can check her out," Sara said.

When we opened the door and my mother saw us, she let out a heavy sigh.

"For god sakes. I'm fine," she spoke.

"Your dizzy spell and near fainting say otherwise. Hi, Caitlin." Sara smiled as she walked over to her.

"Hello, Sara."

"Do you mind if I take a quick look at you?"

"Just do it, Sara. Don't ask her. She doesn't have a choice," I said.

"Excuse me, Mason Matthew Wolfe?" she spoke in a stern voice.

"Why don't you wait outside and let me examine her. Okay?"

"Sure."

I tucked my hands in my pocket and left the room.

"Uncle Mason!" Ruby wrapped her arms around my waist.

"Hey there, Ruby." I patted her head.

"Is Grandma Caitlin going to be okay? I'm worried about her."

I took hold of her hands and knelt down in front of her.

"She'll be fine. She has the best doctor in there with her right now."

I heard the front door open and Elijah's voice, so I walked downstairs to greet him.

"Hey, bro," I spoke.

"Where's Mom? Is she okay?"

"Sara is upstairs checking her out right now. We were having dinner when Allison called."

"Dinner together?" His brow arched.

"Yeah. We're roommates. We're not allowed to have dinner together?"

"Sure. I just thought you two were avoiding each other as much as possible."

"Her shift got switched at the hospital and I came home from the station and we were hungry. Why the hell am I even explaining this to you?" I furrowed my brows.

"I don't know. Why are you?" A smirk crossed his face as he placed his hand on my shoulder.

"Hi, Elijah." Sara smiled as she walked down the stairs.

"Hey, Sara. Thanks for coming over."

"No problem."

"How is she?" I asked.

"She'll be fine after I make her something to eat."

"She's not eating again?" Elijah asked.

"I think maybe you two should go up and talk to her."

As Elijah and I walked up the stairs, I asked him if he talked to Tommy.

"I tried. He's not saying anything. All he said was to talk to Mom."

We opened the door to her room and stepped inside.

"Great. Now all we need is Nathan here." She narrowed her eye at us.

"You don't have to worry about that. He's still at work," I spoke as I sat on the edge of the bed and took hold of her hand.

"What is going on?" Elijah demanded to know.

"Bro, cool it."

"No! I won't cool it. Mother, you will tell us what the hell is going on! Do you understand me?"

"Fine. But it will have to wait until Nathan is here. I want to talk to all three of you together."

"Okay. Then I'll find out when Nathan is available and coordinate our schedules," Elijah spoke.

CHAPTER 15

*S*ara

"Thanks again for your help," Mason said as we climbed into the cab.

"Don't mention it. That's why I'm a doctor." I smiled.

"I just don't understand what is going on. I've never seen her like this before. Are you sure it's not something more serious?"

"It's a matter of her being depressed and not taking care of herself. Maybe once she finally talks to you and your brothers, she'll feel better."

"I hope so." He sighed.

As we stepped into the apartment, I walked over to the table and started cleaning up from dinner while Mason grabbed the beer bottles.

"I have an early shift tomorrow, so I'm going to head to bed."

"I'm off tomorrow." Mason grinned. "Thanks, Sara. I think it's kind of nice having a doctor in the house."

"You're welcome. I'll see you around, Wolfe."

"Good night," he spoke.

&

*M*ason Wolfe, what can I say? He was definitely hot and sexy. And despite his flirtatious nature, he was a really nice guy. He was the kind of guy I didn't need to think dirty thoughts about. We were friends now and roommates and I wouldn't dare cross that line, no matter how horny I was. I didn't need that kind of complication in my life right now.

I took a shower, changed into my nightshirt and climbed in bed, grabbing the remote and my Wii U controller. I had just started playing when I heard a light knock at the door.

"Yes?"

"I hate to ask you this, but could I borrow some toothpaste? I'm out and my other one is at the station."

"Sure. Come on in. It's in the top drawer in the bathroom," I spoke as he opened the door.

"Thanks. You're playing Mario Kart?"

"Yeah. Why? Is that a problem?" I gave him a smirk.

"No. Not at all. I love that game. I kick Nathan's ass every time." He grinned.

"Wanna play? There's another controller on my dresser."

"Seriously? I'd love to."

"Great. Grab the controller and watch me kick your ass."

"Don't underestimate my gaming abilities, sweetheart," he said as he climbed on the bed next to me.

We played for a couple of hours and I beat him in every game except one. And that was only because I let him win to soothe his ego.

"Shit. I can't believe you won again. The next time we're both off, we're having a rematch," he said as he climbed off the bed.

"Deal. But I don't want you crying when I kick your ass again." I smirked.

"Please. You're the one who'll be crying."

"Don't forget the toothpaste on your way out," I said as I pulled the covers over me.

"That's right. Thanks. Goodnight, Sara. Sleep well."

"You too, Mason."

He shut the door, and I reached over and turned off my light. As I lay my head on the pillow and closed my eyes, the only thing I saw was him as I replayed the events of our evening in my mind.

I stumbled into the hospital at six a.m. gripping the cup of coffee I'd brought from home. Not only did I get to bed late, I tossed and turned all night.

"Good morning, Sara." Corinne smiled.

"Morning. I wouldn't say it was good."

"What's wrong? Late night?" She smirked.

"Yeah." I sighed. "Not only did I get to bed late, but I didn't sleep very well." I took a sip of my coffee.

"Any particular reason you got to bed late? Like the reason being the sexy firefighter you live with?" Her brow raised.

"No, of course not." I furrowed my brows.

"So what's it like?"

"What is what like?"

"Living with the sexy Captain Mason Wolfe. You're the talk among all the nurses, you know."

"It's all good. We barely see each other. So all of you can stop talking about me." I smirked.

"But we're jealous," she whined as I walked away. "We want stories that involve juicy details. We all just want to live vicariously through you! By the way, we're all going to Rudy's after our shift. Are you up for a little drinking tonight?"

"Sure." I turned my head with a smile as I walked into exam room three.

My shift ended at six p.m., but by the time I changed my clothes and freshened myself up, it was almost seven.

"Are you ready?" Corinne asked as she walked into the locker room.

"As ready as I'll ever be," I spoke as I smacked my lips together after applying a tinted gloss.

The four of us walked into Rudy's and took a seat at an open table. We ordered our drinks and then the ladies started grilling me about Mason.

"So, Dr. Davis, tell us what it's like living with Captain Mason Wolfe." Audrey grinned.

I sighed as the waitress set our drinks in front of us.

"It's not a big deal. We barely see each other."

"Is he neat or messy?" Corinne asked.

"He's neat. We have rules."

I couldn't believe I was having this conversation with them. They were behaving like teenage girls.

"Does he walk around in his underwear?" Riley asked with a grin.

"Not that I've seen. Like I said, we barely see each other."

There was no way I would tell them we had dinner together or the fact that we played Mario Kart on my bed. We kicked back a few drinks, had some laughs, and then I headed home.

When I opened the door and stepped inside, I saw Mason wasn't home. I knew he wasn't working today, so he was probably out with his brothers or his buddies from the station. After taking a shower and climbing into bed, I fell asleep until I was woken up by the sound of the front door shutting and a lot of giggling. Climbing out of bed, I quietly opened my door a crack and saw Mason and some chick making out as they headed to his room. A feeling I didn't like erupted inside me. Getting back into bed, I lay there and tossed and turned the rest of the night.

The next morning, after I showered and got dressed, I went to grab a cup of coffee when I saw that girl from last night making herself a cup.

"Oh hey." She smiled as she stood there in one of Mason's t-shirts. "You must be the roommate. I'm Candi with an i."

"Hey." I nodded as I reached up in the cabinet and grabbed a cup.

Mason emerged from his room in a pair of sweatpants and stopped dead in his tracks when he saw me.

"Hey," he nervously spoke. "I thought you worked today."

"I do. But not until noon."

"Here you go, baby." Candi grinned as she handed Mason a cup of coffee.

"Thanks. You should go get dressed. I have errands to run."

"Sure. Okay." She ran her hand down his bare chest.

After making myself a cup of coffee, I grabbed the bottle of aspirin and shook two pills in my hand.

"Headache?" Mason asked.

"I drank a little too much last night," I replied as I chased the pills down with a glass of water.

"Oh. Where did you go?"

"Rudy's."

Candi walked back into the kitchen and handed Mason a piece of paper.

"I had a lot of fun last night. Call me."

"Yeah, sure." He gave her a small smile as he took the paper from her hand and I rolled my eyes.

She left and Mason walked over to the fridge and took out the carton of eggs, but not before throwing her number in the garbage.

"I bet you don't even know her name," I spoke.

"Yes, I do. It's—It's—Kathy."

"It's Candi with an i." My brow arched.

"Yes. Right." He nodded. "I hope this isn't awkward for you."

"Nope. Not awkward at all. I just hope the same goes for you when I bring a guy home."

My phone rang, and it was the hospital calling.

"I'm on my way," I spoke as I ended the call. "I have to go. The ER is getting slammed. There's a twenty-car pileup on the expressway."

CHAPTER 16

*M*ason

She flew out the door, and I sat there wondering if she had heard us last night. I couldn't worry about it because this was my place too, and if I wanted to bring someone back for the night, I would with no guilt. This was the problem with having a roommate. Especially one that was a woman. I needed to stop worrying about it. Just as I got up to change in my running clothes, there was a knock at the door. Opening it, Nathan stood there with his head cocked.

"Why the hell aren't you ready? I thought we were going for a run?"

"We are. Come on in. Let me go throw on some clothes," I spoke as I rubbed the back of my neck.

"What's wrong?"

"Nothing."

"Bullshit," he shouted from the living room. "I've known you my entire life, and I know that look. What happened?"

After changing into my running shorts and t-shirt, I took my socks and shoes over to the couch.

"I brought a girl home last night and her and Sara saw each other this morning."

"And?"

"And it was a little awkward."

"Why? You and Sara aren't having sex. You're not a couple. You're roommates. Did she have a problem with it?"

"I don't think so." I got up from the couch. "I told her I hoped it wasn't awkward for her and she said it wasn't and that she hopes I would feel the same when she brought a guy home."

"There you have it." He patted my shoulder. "She didn't feel awkward, you won't feel awkward, everything will be dandy and now we can go for our run." He grinned.

I rolled my eyes as I grabbed my phone and we headed out the door.

"Do you think Mom will tell us everything tonight?" Nathan asked as we ran through Central Park.

"She better. Maybe we should force her to get some counseling."

"Seriously? You don't force Mom to do anything. She forces us to do the things we don't want to."

"True." I smiled. "Well, whatever happened between her and Tommy, we'll find out tonight."

﹩

I stepped into the townhouse and found Elijah and Nathan in the living room kicking back a scotch.

"Where's Mom?" I asked.

"She'll be down in a second. Scotch?" Elijah asked.

"Sure. Thanks."

"How is the living situation going?" he asked.

"It's—"

"Our little brother brought a girl home last night and her and Sara ran into each other this morning and now he's feeling guilty about it." Nathan smirked.

"I am not, douchebag."

"You two aren't sleeping together or dating, so why would you feel guilty?" Elijah asked.

"I don't feel guilty. It was just a little awkward. I don't know," I spoke as Elijah handed me my scotch.

"Good, you're all here," My mother said as she walked into the living room. "The three of you may sit down, and I'll explain everything."

The three of us took our seats. To be honest, I'd never seen my mother this nervous.

"I broke up with Tommy because he asked me to marry him."

"Wouldn't a simple 'no' have sufficed?" Nathan asked.

"I said no and then I broke up with him."

"Mom, you love Tommy. At least that's what we all thought," I said.

"I do love him, and I miss him terribly."

"Then what's the problem?" Elijah asked.

"I was married once, and it destroyed me. I am not about to let that happen again in my lifetime. Plus, he's younger than me and as I grow old, he'll decide one day to seek someone either his own age or younger."

"You don't know that, Mom," I said.

"Listen," Elijah spoke as he got up from the couch and hooked his arm around her. "Isn't 'not' being with him destroying you? We have never seen you like this before. Tommy is a good man, and he deserves you in his life. And you deserve a man like him. Don't let your fears stop you from being happy. No one can predict what will happen in the future, so isn't being happy in the now more important than worrying about what might happen?"

"I'm saving myself from the pain and heartache."

"And you're doing such a good job at it," Nathan spoke, and I smacked his arm.

"Mom, Tommy makes you happy. You have never been with a guy as long as you have with him. That has to mean something," I said as I got up and took hold of her hand.

"Yeah, Mom. You love him, he loves you, and it's time you grow up and let yourself be happy," Nathan said. "Stop worrying so much about what could happen and love where you're at right now. I mean, when you were with Tommy. We like the guy. He's good for you and he's good for us."

"Good for me how, Nathan?" My mother asked as she raised her brow.

"He keeps you occupied so you don't have time to interfere in our lives." He grinned.

"I will always interfere in your lives. It's my job and duty as a mother, so get used to it."

"Here," Elijah said as he picked up her phone from the coffee table and handed it to her. "Call, invite him over, and tell him all your fears. Don't shut him out. He doesn't deserve that."

"I'm scared. What if he never wants to see me again?"

"He does. He's just as broken up as you are," Elijah spoke.

The three of us left the room and let her make the call.

"Damn. I never thought we'd be having a conversation like that with her," I said.

"That's because she never truly cared for someone after dad," Elijah chimed in.

"Do you think they'll get back together?" Nathan asked.

"I think so. If not, the three of us will be ready to go to his house and smack some sense into him." Elijah smirked.

"Well?" I asked my mother as she walked into the kitchen.

"He's on his way over. You boys better get going."

"See, Mom. No worries." Nathan smiled as he kissed her cheek.

"I'm happy for you, Mom. You're doing the right thing." I gave her a hug.

CHAPTER 17

*S*ara

By the time I got off work and headed home, it was after ten o'clock. When I walked through the door of the apartment, I saw Mason in the kitchen grabbing a beer from the fridge.

"Hey," I said as I set down my purse and bag.

"Hey. You look like you could use a beer." He smiled.

"Sounds good. I'm exhausted."

"Tough day in the ER?"

"Yes. Between that accident this morning and everybody in the city thinking they're dying, it was really busy," I said as I kicked off my shoes and sat on the couch.

He let out a chuckle as he twisted off the cap and handed me my beer.

"How was your day?" I asked as he sat down next to me and put his feet up on the coffee table.

"It was good. I just got back from my mother's house. She told us why she broke up with Tommy."

"Good. Hopefully after letting it all out to you boys, she'll start to feel better."

"He asked her to marry him."

"What?" I cocked my head. "She broke up with him because he wants to marry her?"

"Yep. She never got over my father leaving. It's always been one short term guy after the other over the years. It's what we expected from her. It's just how it's always been. And I think my mom thought the same. But each time we saw them together, we knew he was something special to her, and she did too. But we talked some sense into her, and she called him. He was on his way over when we left."

"You know, I've never seen brothers as close as the three of you are. You're all very protective of one another and of your mother and I think it's amazing. Now hopefully, I won't be seeing your mom in my ER anymore."

"Hopefully not." He held up his beer bottle and I tipped mine to his.

"I envy your family."

"Believe me, we have plenty of issues. It's not always perfect."

"Can I ask you a personal question. If I'm overstepping, just tell me."

"What do you want to ask me?"

"I know you're a captain and you make decent money—"

"But how would I have afforded this place on my own?" He smirked.

"Yes." I pointed at him.

"After we were born, my grandparents, who were extremely wealthy, set up trust funds and made investments in our name. I'm pretty much set for life. The money I make from the fire department is spending money." He winked.

"Ah, how nice."

"And you?" His brow arched. "I know you'll make good money in time, but you just finished your residency."

"I don't have any student loans and I lived at home. So, I really don't have any debt except a couple of credit cards. Don't get me wrong. I really didn't want to pay this much for rent, but it felt like home and it was convenient."

"Does it still feel like home?" he asked as our eyes locked onto each other's.

"Yeah. It does." A soft smile crossed my lips.

I swallowed hard as I stared into his mesmerizing eyes. I was horny and he was here, sitting right next to me looking sexy as fuck, like he always did.

"I'm going to head to bed," I said as I got up from the couch and set my empty beer bottle on the counter.

"Me too. I have to be at the station early tomorrow morning. I'm starting a thirty-six-hour shift, so I won't be home."

"Okay. Maybe I'll see you at the hospital."

"Yeah. Maybe. Goodnight, Sara. I hope you sleep well," he said as he headed towards his room.

"Goodnight, Mason."

For one split second, I contemplated smashing my mouth against his. But the fleeting thought left as quickly as it came. Sex can do either one of two things: it can strengthen a relationship, or it can ruin one. We hadn't lived together very long, and we were just starting a friendship. But damn if I didn't get turned on every time he looked at me.

*

I hadn't seen or talked to Mason in three days. As much as I craved and loved living alone, I missed his company. Even if it was little bits and pieces at a time. I had just ended my shift at the hospital, and by time I got home it was seven p.m. When I walked through the door, I saw Nathan and Mason sitting at the table drinking beer and eating pizza.

"Hey." I smiled as I walked in and set my purse down.

"Hey, Sara," both of them spoke at the same time.

"There's plenty of pizza here if you're hungry," Mason said.

"Thanks. I'm starving."

I opened the refrigerator, grabbed a beer and took it over to the table.

"I got a text from your mom today. She asked me if I worked tomorrow and when I told her it was my day off, she invited me to your family dinner."

"Really?" Mason asked.

"Wow," Nathan spoke as he took a bite of his pizza. "She must consider you a part of the family now. The more the merrier." He grinned.

"Are you going?" Mason asked.

"You better come. Nobody turns down an invite from Caitlin Wolfe," Nathan said. "Trust me, you don't want to get on her bad side."

"I guess I could go. If that's okay with you, Mason."

"Yeah. Sure." He took a sip of his beer.

"I better get going, bro. Thanks for the beer and pizza. I'll see you tomorrow night. And I'll see you there as well." Nathan smiled as he pointed at me.

Mason collected the beer bottles and took them over to the sink.

"Are you sure you don't mind me joining your family for dinner tomorrow? I can always tell your mom I already have other plans."

"It's fine. Like Nathan said, you don't want to get on her bad side."

"You seem bothered she invited me," I spoke as I got up from the table and grabbed the pizza box.

"I'm not bothered. I just find it a little strange because family dinner has always been just for family. It makes me wonder what she's up to."

"You're right. I'm not family and I shouldn't be there. Just tell her I couldn't make it." I turned away and started walking to my room.

Suddenly, I felt his hand grip my arm.

"I didn't mean it like that, Sara." His eyes stared into mine. "I want you to come tomorrow."

"Okay. Goodnight, Mason."

"Goodnight."

I went to my room, shut the door and leaned against it as I took in a deep breath.

CHAPTER 18

*M*ason

What the hell was my mother thinking by inviting Sara to our family dinner? It was bad enough we lived together, and I had to control the strong sexual attraction I felt towards her. I was sitting at the island drinking my coffee when she walked over to the cabinet in her short nightshirt that barely covered her ass as she reached up to grab a cup. My cock twitched, and if I didn't do something quick, I'd be hard in a matter of seconds.

"Good morning," I said.

"Morning." She turned around and flashed me a smile before popping in a k-cup into the Keurig.

"How did you sleep?" I asked.

"Great." She grinned as she took her coffee and went to her bedroom.

I sighed as I got up from my seat and took a shower. When I finished, I got dressed and noted how quiet the apartment seemed. Walking out into the living area, I called Sara's name. No answer. So I knocked on the door to her bedroom and waited. When she didn't answer, I slowly opened the door and looked inside. She wasn't in there.

After meeting two of my buddies from the station for lunch, I ran some errands and headed back to the apartment. Sara still wasn't home. It was five o'clock, and we needed to be at my mother's house at six. Pulling out my phone, I sent her a text message.

"Family dinner is at six o'clock."

"I know. I'll be there by six."

I stared at her message in confusion because I thought we were going together, but I guess she had other plans.

❧

"*H*ello, darling." My mother smiled as I stepped into the kitchen.

"Hey, Mom." I kissed her on the cheek.

"Where's Sara?"

"She's on her way."

"You two didn't come together?"

"No. She was out all day."

I walked into the living room where I saw Elijah holding Mila and talking to Tommy.

"Hey, Tommy." I shook his hand. "Good to see you again."

"You too, Mason." A smile crossed his face. "If you boys will excuse me, I'm going to see if your mother needs any help in the kitchen."

"Hey, pretty girl." I held out my arms to Mila. "It's good to see Tommy back in the picture."

"Yeah. What a difference. Mom was in the best mood today. It was kind of weird."

"Speaking of weird, did you know Mom invited Sara to dinner?"

"Yeah. She told me. I don't think it's weird. She is your roommate." He turned and poured himself another scotch. "Scotch?"

"No thanks. She's not family, bro."

"Apparently, Mom thinks she is since the two of you are living together."

"Where's Aspen?" I asked as I set Mila down.

"She's on her way. She got tied up with a client."

"And Nathan?"

"I'm right here, douchebag." He slapped me on the back of the head.

"Bro, knock it off." I punched his arm.

"Boys, dinner is ready," my mother spoke from the foyer.

"Where's Sara?" Nathan whispered in my ear. "Did she change her mind?"

"No. She said she'll meet me here."

Just as I said that, there was a knock at the door. When I opened it, Sara stood there holding a white box.

"Hey."

"Hey." She smiled as she stepped inside. "I brought a pie."

"My mother will love that." I took the box from her. "Thanks."

"Sara, darling. I'm so happy you could make it," my mother spoke as she gave her a light hug.

"Thanks for inviting me, Caitlin."

"Dinner is ready so everyone take your seats in the dining room."

I escorted Sara to the table, and she took the empty seat next to mine while my mother and Tommy both stood at the head of the table.

"I've brought all of you here tonight—"

"I'm so sorry I'm late. I got tied up with a client," Aspen spoke as she dashed into the dining room, kissed Mila on the head, Elijah on the cheek, and took her seat next to him.

"It's okay, darling. Now that everyone in my beautiful family is here, Tommy and I have an announcement to make," she spoke as she took his hand. "We're getting married."

The room buzzed with excitement as we all stood up from our seats and congratulated them.

"When?" I asked.

"Next weekend in Las Vegas, and you're all coming with us. It worked out best because all of you are off work, including you, Sara. I've already booked the private jet and made the reservations for the rooms. Mason, you and Sara will share a two-bedroom suite since you're already roommates."

I glanced at Sara, who looked at me as she bit down on her bottom lip.

"Now, let's eat," my mother said as she and Tommy took their seats.

After we ate, I walked into the living room and poured myself a scotch.

"You are so screwed," Nathan whispered in my ear as he hooked his arm around me.

"What are you talking about?"

"Mom royally screwed you with the room situation in Vegas. How the hell are you supposed to bring hot chicks back to the room with Sara there?"

"I don't want to talk about it." I walked away.

It was bad enough I felt like I couldn't bring anyone back to the apartment, and now she had to ruin Vegas for me.

"What's wrong, little brother?" Elijah asked as he walked up to me.

"Mom. That's what's wrong. Why the hell would she invite Sara to Vegas? Or better yet, why would she stick us in the same suite?"

"Um, bro?" Nathan spoke.

When I looked over, I saw Sara standing there with a look of hurt on her face. She quickly turned away and walked out the door.

"Shit!"

"Bro, you better go after her," Nathan said. "Because if you don't, there will be a hell of a lot of tension at home tonight and tomorrow, and probably for the rest of the time you're living together."

"Nathan's right, Mason. You hurt her and you need to fix it."

After I said goodbye to my mom and Tommy, I left.

CHAPTER 19

S ara
    I flew out the front door and hastily walked down the street and around the corner. It was obvious he didn't want me going to Vegas with them, just like it was obvious he didn't want me at dinner. The hurt and humiliation I felt was out of control.

I hailed a cab to Central Park, took a seat on the bench and watched as the joggers ran by. Thousands of scenarios went through my head about how he would try and explain himself when I got home, but I didn't owe it to him to listen. In fact, I didn't owe him anything at all. I heard what I heard and the irritated tone he said it in. I was a strong woman who had endured so much bullshit in life, and I wasn't about to let a man named Mason Wolfe bring me down. He had his life, and I had mine and it was best we kept our lives separate.

After sitting in Central Park for a couple hours, darkness had settled in and I headed home. When I walked through the door, I saw Mason sitting on the couch scrolling through his phone.

"Where were you?" he asked in an irritated tone.

"Out."

I headed to my bedroom, and as I went to shut the door, he stopped it with his hand.

"Excuse me?" I turned and shot him a look.

"We need to talk."

"Okay. I'll do the talking and then this conversation will be over. You don't have to worry about me going to Vegas with you and your family, because I'm not. You don't have to worry about me infringing on your little get-togethers anymore, because I won't. There, discussion over. Now leave."

I went to shut the door, and he stopped it, again.

"Nah, sweetheart, it's not over. Not until I apologize."

"Oh. You mean lie?" My brow arched. "I heard what you said and the way you said it. You can't apologize for something you truly mean. Just fucking admit it, Mason. You don't want me hanging around with you and your family. It's completely fine. I didn't ask to. Your mother is the one who asked me, and I can see it bothers you, so I'm out."

"Do you want to know why?" he asked.

"Frankly, I don't care." I pushed past him and went to the kitchen.

"You don't feel it, Sara?" he shouted as he gripped my arm and spun me around.

"Feel what?" I spoke through gritted teeth.

"The sexual tension between us? My god, it's all I can think about. And every time you're around it gets worse. It's frustrating the fuck out of me. It's bad enough I have to see you here and then my mom goes and invites you to our family dinner and now Vegas!"

"Then let me set things straight with her. I will call her and tell her I can't go because you're too sexually frustrated." I narrowed my eye at him when all I wanted to do was smash my mouth into his.

"You wouldn't dare." His grip on my arm tightened.

"Try me," I spoke with my narrowed eye.

Before I knew it, his mouth was on mine. I should have fought and pushed him away, but I couldn't. The feel of his silky lips on mine felt too good as did the fire that erupted down below. His tongue met mine, and I was done for. He abruptly stopped and stared into my eyes.

"I'm sorry. I shouldn't have—"

74

"Yes, you should have." I gripped the bottom of my shirt and lifted it over my head.

He placed his hands on each side of my face and smashed his mouth into mine once again.

"My room or yours?" he asked as he broke our kiss long enough to take off his shirt.

"Yours is closer." I smiled.

He picked me up, and I wrapped my legs tightly around him as he carried me to his room. We both fell onto the bed as our lips locked in a passionate kiss, and my hands explored his chiseled chest. His fingers unbuttoned my pants and his hands pulled them from my hips as his tongue traveled down my torso. The heat that erupted inside me was unbearable as my skin trembled at his touch. As I watched him take down his pants, I swallowed hard at the large bulge and impatiently waited as he took down his underwear, releasing his hard cock that stood tall and thick. Reaching into his nightstand, he pulled out a condom and threw it on the bed before hovering over me and planting his lips on mine. With one hand, he reached behind me and unclasped my bra with finesse. Taking it from me, he threw it over the side of the bed and deftly ran the back of his hand around my breast before taking my hardened peak in his mouth. Letting out a moan, I could feel the wetness emerge from me.

CHAPTER 20

*M*ason

She had the perfect body, and I wanted to explore every inch of her. My hand slid down her torso and down the front of her pink lace panties. Her freshly shaved pussy was wet as fuck. As much as I loved tasting her lips, I had other areas to taste. Making my way down to her sweet spot, I circled her clit with my tongue, taking in the sweet taste that turned me on even more. Her hands combed through my hair as light moans escaped her lips. She arched her back, begging for me to go deeper. I obliged and before long, she orgasmed. It was incredibly sexy, and I needed to be inside her.

Reaching over and grabbing the condom, I tore the package, rolled it over my cock and slowly thrust inside her as we both let out pleasurable moans. She welcomed every inch of me and soon, I was buried deep inside her. Holding her arms above her head, I thrust in and out as our lips entwined, and my heart rapidly beat as I felt the pressure building up. Not only for me, but for her as well. Several moans escaped us as I let go of her wrists and felt the tips of her nails dig into the flesh of my back as we moved together effortlessly. Slowing my thrust, I buried myself deep inside her as my cock exploded with pleasure. Dropping my body on hers, I could feel the warmth of her bated breath against my neck.

Once my heart rate slowed, I climbed off her and rolled on my back, taking the condom off and throwing it in the trash can next to the bed.

"As amazing as that was, we don't need to talk about it, right?" she asked as she glanced over at me.

"No. Not if you don't want to."

"Okay. I'm going to my room now."

"You're welcome to stay here tonight. I promise we won't talk about it." I smirked.

"Thanks, but I think it's best that I sleep in my own bed."

"Okay. If you change your mind, I'll be here."

She gave me a small smile and a nod, climbed out of bed and grabbed her clothes. Placing my hands behind my head, I watched as her perfectly naked body walked out of my room. Damn. I was still hard, which was unusual for me. She didn't want to talk about what happened between us, but at some point, we'd have to. We couldn't live together and pretend it never happened. I closed my eyes to try to get some sleep, but I couldn't pause the replay that was happening in my head.

🐚

*T*he next morning, I got up at the crack of dawn and met my brothers at the gym. By the time I got there, Nathan and Elijah were already warming up by the weight bench, so I grabbed a twenty-five-pound plate and joined them.

"Good morning. You look like shit." Elijah smirked.

"Thanks. I love you too, bro."

"How did it go last night with Sara?" Nathan asked. "You still in the doghouse?"

"I never was in the doghouse, douchebag. We aren't together."

"Then let me rephrase that. Are you still in the friendship doghouse?"

77

"No. She came home last night, and we talked." I looked away as I finished warming up.

Elijah narrowed his eye at me as he took a seat on the bench.

"What?"

"You slept with her."

"No—Well—"

"I knew it!" Nathan pointed at me. "Pay up, bro." He held his hand out to Elijah.

Elijah shook his head, reached in his pocket, pulled out a fifty-dollar bill and handed it to Nathan.

"What the fuck!" I said. "You two had a bet?"

"I told Elijah your fight would lead to sex, and he disagreed, so we made a little wager." Nathan grinned.

"So now what?" Elijah asked.

"Nothing," Nathan chimed in. "He got what he wanted and now he'll move on. Right, bro?" He hooked his arm around me. "But now you've gone and made things awkward because the two of you have to see each other every day."

"It's not awkward. We fucked, she went to her bed, I stayed in mine and that's it."

"What did you do, kick her out of your bed after doing the dirty deed?" Nathan asked.

"No. She wanted to go. I'm done talking about this."

"Sounds to me like she regretted it," Elijah said as he lifted his weights.

"Do you?" Nathan asked.

"No. Shit happens. We fucked, got it out of the way, and now we can move on."

"Good luck with that," Nathan said. "She's not your typical one-night stand, bro. Have you forgotten the TWO of you live together?"

"Both of you drop it. I'm heading over to the cable pull machine."

CHAPTER 21

*S*ara

I'd barely slept all night as I stumbled out of bed and went to the kitchen for a cup of coffee.

"Good. He was still asleep." I thought to myself.

I didn't have to be at work until one and hiding in my room until then was the plan. How could I face him after what happened last night? My body still tingled at the sensation every time I thought about it. It was an incredible experience and exactly what I'd needed. We had rules, and we broke them. As I was pondering my thoughts, the door opened, and Mason walked in. Shit.

"Hey. Good morning." He smiled as he set a white bag down on the island.

"Morning." I gripped my coffee cup tightly between my hands.

"I bought us some bagels. I wasn't sure if you worked or not today."

"I don't go in until one."

"Great. Then sit down and have one," he said as he grabbed the cream cheese from the fridge.

He was acting like last night was no big deal. Maybe for him it wasn't, but for me it was. Typical guy.

"That's okay. Maybe I'll have one later," I said as I began to walk away.

"Sara."

"Yeah." I turned around.

"Sit down now," his authoritative voice spoke. "You love bagels and I know you want one."

I sighed as I walked over to the island and took a seat.

"Listen," he said as he took a bagel out of the bag and began spreading it with cream cheese. "We have to talk about last night. There's no getting around it. To be honest, I think you're making a big deal out of nothing."

"No, I'm not."

"Yes, you are." He smiled as he set my bagel in front of me. "We had sex. Big deal. Have you never had a one-night stand before?"

"Of course, I have!"

"Then how is what happened between us any different? Come on, we both knew it was inevitable, and you can't say otherwise."

He was right. It was inevitable, and in the back of my mind I knew it.

"You're right. It just feels different because we live together and see each other all the time."

He shrugged.

"It will only be awkward if we let it be. But we're both mature adults who just see it as casual sex and no big deal. We're friends, and I'm sorry I hurt your feelings last night. It's not that I don't want you hanging with my family, I do. They love you and that makes me happy. I was just frustrated about our situation."

"And now you're not?" I arched my brow.

"No. I'm not."

"Okay. Good. Then today is a new day and we'll just move forward. You're right. No big deal. It was just amazing casual sex." I smiled.

"Yeah. It was amazing." He smiled back.

As busy as I was at the hospital, it didn't stop my mind from thinking about Mason and the sex we'd had. It was invigorating and beyond the best sex I'd ever had in my life. I thought a lot about things I shouldn't have. Things that would ultimately lead me down a path of destruction, but only if I let it. I was strong, and I was a fighter. I'd spent so many years in medical school, taking care of myself and taking care of my mom, that it was time to put me first. I wasn't looking for a relationship because I still didn't trust men. Would I ever? Who the hell knew? But one thing was certain, I enjoyed our evening together; he wasn't looking for anything, and I craved more.

I pulled out my phone and sent Mason a text message.

"I get off at nine o'clock. If you're going to be home tonight, how about a game of Mario Kart?"

"I guess I could stick around to kick your ass."

"We'll see about that, Mr. Wolfe. Game on. Better use your off time to practice before I get home."

"Turning the game on as we speak. I'll see you later."

⅋

"Can I ask you a question?" I said as we sat on the couch and played our game.

"Sure."

"How do you feel about friends with benefits?"

He paused the game and looked at me.

"I don't really know. I've never had a friend with benefits. You?"

"I never had one either."

"I suppose it could be fun. Are you suggesting that me and you—"

"Maybe." I bit down on my bottom lip.

"Oh." His brow arched.

"Okay. It was a stupid idea," I said as I got up from the couch and grabbed two beers from the fridge.

"No. It's not a stupid idea at all. I'm just surprised you would want that."

"Why?" I handed him his beer. "I have needs and believe it or not, I have a big sexual appetite."

"Damn. Really?" He grinned.

"Yes. Sometimes I think I was supposed to be born a guy."

He chuckled.

"You know I don't trust guys and I'm not looking for anything else besides sex. To be honest, I trust you enough for that."

"Dr. Sara Davis." He smirked. "I knew there was a wild side to you."

"Stop it. This is hard enough as it is."

"Trust me. It's hard all right."

"Mason." I smacked his arm as I sat down next to him. "I'm serious."

"So am I, Sara. Look." He pointed to his cock.

Sure as shit, he was sporting a rock solid hard on.

"I'm in if you are." He grinned.

"We'll need rules first," I said as I sipped my beer.

"Rules, rules, rules. We will come up with a set as soon as I take care of this hard on."

He set his beer on the coffee table and took mine from my hand. Bringing his hand up to my cheek, he softly brushed his lips against mine.

CHAPTER 22

Mason

I thrust in and out of her from behind as she held onto the back of the couch. Her moans heightened my sexual excitement while she came. I pulled out of her and sat down, bringing her on top. She guided my cock inside her and quickly took in every inch of me. The pleasure was so intense it sent my eyes to the back of my head. She rode me without fear and without hesitation. This woman was on fire, and I loved every second of it. She let loose on me and it felt amazing. She had another orgasm, and just as I was about to come, I gripped her hips and held them down as I exploded inside her. She wrapped her arms around me as I held her in place. Our skin melted with sweat and our hearts rapidly beat. I could feel her erratic breathing on my neck as she could feel mine on hers. She climbed off me and fell onto the couch.

"Fuck." I smiled as I glanced over at her, trying to regain my breath.

"Yes, we did." She grinned.

I removed the condom, got up and threw it in the garbage.

"I'm going to clean up and get in my pajamas. I'll be right back and then we'll discuss the rules."

"Anything you say, sweetheart."

I grabbed my clothes from the floor, took them into my room and grabbed a pair of sweatpants from my drawer. After slipping into them, I went back out to the living room, grabbed my beer from the table and brought the bottle up to my lips.

"Okay. I made a list of potential rules," she said as she sat down on the couch with a piece of paper in her hand.

"Did you just write those down now?"

"No. I worked on them all day in between patients just in case you said yes."

"Wow. Okay. Let's hear them."

"Like I said, these are only potential rules that we will thoroughly discuss. If something doesn't sound right to you or you disagree with any of them, we'll talk about it."

"Got it." I smiled.

"Okay. Rule number one. We both need to be very clear about what we're looking for and what we're not looking for. I think transparency is a must in this situation."

"I agree. I'm not looking for anything other than sex. I don't want a relationship, commitment, nothing. Just sex and friendship," I said.

"That's exactly the way I feel, Mason. I want nothing other than great sex."

"Not a problem." I gave her a wink. "What's the next rule?"

"I think it's important that we check in with each other periodically about how we feel about our 'friends with benefits' relationship. Is it working for us? Are there any issues we need to work out?"

"Good idea. Open and honest. I like it."

"The next rule is how will we keep our newfound friendship? Are we going to tell people about it? Or agree to keep it between ourselves?"

"I don't think it's anyone's business what we do. So I think we should keep it to ourselves," I said.

"That includes your brothers." Her brow arched.

"I know and trust me, they do not need to know about our arrangement."

"We're doing this just to have fun and enjoy each other physically, right?" she asked.

"Definitely."

"Okay. As long as we're both clear on that. As for the ultimate rule, if one of us should meet someone and it becomes serious, we need to talk to each other about it."

"That's fine, but I don't have any plans on seriously meeting anyone. Seriousness isn't my thing." I finished off my beer.

"You never know, Mason."

"Trust me, sweetheart, I am not a serious relationship type of guy. Never have been and never will be."

"I'm sure your brothers said the same thing."

"They did, but they're weak. I'm like them in certain ways, but nothing like them in others. I have my own set of beliefs that are set in stone for me."

"Okay. That wraps up the rules then. I will make a copy for you to tuck away in your drawer, just in case you need reminding."

"Sounds good. You're coming to Vegas, right?"

"Do you really want me to?"

"I do." I smiled as I took hold of her hand. "With our newfound friendship and rules, we're going to have a blast."

"Then I'll come."

I leaned over and planted a kiss on her lips.

"Um, is random kissing allowed?" I asked.

"Sure. I like random friend kisses."

*V*egas was a blast, and I couldn't wrap my head around the fact that my mother was married. To each his own, I guess. Sara and I had been in our friends with benefits zone for two months and what a whirlwind it was. My brothers hadn't a clue what was going on, and that's how I planned to keep it. I was having fun, plenty of sex and enjoying life. Then one night, after a round of sex with Sara, I found myself not wanting her to leave my bed.

"Stay," I said as I grabbed her hand before she got up from the bed.

"What? Why?"

"Why not? We haven't slept together in the same bed yet. I was thinking we could wake up together and have morning sex while we were still in bed. Sleeping in the same bed means nothing, Sara."

"I guess you're right. Okay." She climbed back under the covers.

I wrapped my arms around her and closed my eyes.

CHAPTER 23

*S*ara

I purposely never stayed in bed with him for a reason. The reason being because I was afraid to get too close. We were having fun, and I was letting some emotions run high. Emotions such as missing him when he was at work or out with his friends. We were over two months into our arrangement, and I was already starting to break the rules. I was falling for him. Hell, I'd already fell. I thought this would be no big deal, but the more time I spent with him, the more I trusted him. We just didn't have sex all the time. We played games; we went grocery shopping together when we were both home, and we'd listen to the same music. He'd break out his guitar and strum a tune, and we'd both sing the lyrics together. I considered him my best friend, and it scared the hell out of me. But I wouldn't tell him for fear he'd end our arrangement. So for now, I needed to keep silent, breaking one of my own rules.

Lying there, wrapped up in his muscular arms, made me feel safe. A feeling I hadn't felt in many years. There was only one man in my life once upon a time that made me feel the way Mason did, and he was my father. But all that went out the window and set me on a path of loneliness and unsureness the day the ugly truth came out.

I had my alarm set for five a.m. for I needed to be at the hospital by seven. Reaching over to shut it off, Mason tightened his grip around me.

"Good morning," he sleepily spoke as his lips pressed against the flesh of my back.

"Morning." I turned in his arms.

"What time is it?"

"It's five. I need to be at the hospital by seven."

"And I need to be at the fire station by eight." He sighed.

"You still have some time to sleep. I'm going to take a shower."

"Sounds good to me." He rolled over.

I sat on the edge of the bed for a moment and stared at him. This all sounded easy when I proposed the idea. Now, it had just become complicated.

৯▲

*M*ason

She left the bedroom, and I turned on my back and placed my arm behind my head. Sleeping with and holding her all night felt — Hell, I didn't know. I liked it and I didn't want her to leave. If there was one thing I knew for sure, it was I enjoyed being with her. And not just sexually. I enjoyed being with her period. Life always seemed to be better when she was around.

I was only working an eight-hour shift because I'd agreed to cover another firefighter's shift. It was the least I could do since I owed him a favor. But even if I didn't owe him a favor, I still would have done it because that's what we did. We always had each other's backs.

It was a rare quiet day. When my shift ended, I headed over to Rudy's.

"Hey, Mason. You here alone?"

"Hi, Hanna. Yeah. I just stopped in for a quick drink, then I'm heading home."

"What are you drinking tonight?"

"Give me a scotch and make it a double."

"Coming right up." She smiled.

As I was drinking my scotch, an older gentleman sat down on the stool next to me. I glanced over at him, gave him a nod, and then went back to my drink.

"What can I get you?" Hanna asked him.

"I'll have what he's having," the gentleman spoke. "Thank you for your service," he said as he glanced over at me.

"Excuse me?"

"I see you're a firefighter." He pointed to the logo on my sleeve. "And a captain. Impressive."

"Yeah." I smiled. "Thanks."

"Is that something you always wanted to do?" he asked.

"Ever since I could remember." I smiled.

"That's one hell of a dangerous job." He took a sip of his scotch.

"You sound like my mother. She's always trying to get me to switch careers."

He let out a chuckle.

"I'm not surprised. Moms are always overprotective. But the important thing is to do what you love and what makes you happy, regardless of the danger."

"Trust me. I am, and this is one battle my mom won't win. What do you do?"

"I'm retired. I just got into New York a week ago."

"Oh yeah. Where are you from?" I held up my glass to Hanna to let her know I needed a refill.

"Alaska. I was a commercial fisherman."

"Crab?" I arched my brow.

"Yep." The corners of his mouth curved upward.

"Talk about a dangerous job."

"One of the deadliest." He grinned as he brought his glass up to his lips.

"Wow. I bet you have some great stories."

"I do. I'll tell them to you sometime."

"By the way, I'm Mason." I held out my hand.

"Nice to meet you, Mason. I'm Jack." He shook my hand.

"So, what brings you to New York?" I asked. "Do you have family here?"

"Nah, no family. I came here for personal reasons. You're actually the first person here I've met. I better get going." He finished his drink. "I don't want to overstay my welcome here." He threw some cash down on the bar and got up from his stool. "It was nice to meet you, Mason."

As he walked away, I shouted his name.

"Hey, Jack?"

"Yeah?" He turned around.

"How would you like to come to dinner at my place tomorrow night? I know it must be hard not knowing anyone here."

"That's very kind of you, but I don't want to impose."

"If I thought you were imposing, I wouldn't have asked. Say around seven?" I asked Hanna for a pen and wrote my address on a napkin and handed it to him.

"Seven sounds good. I'll be there." The corners of his mouth curved upward. "You're a good man, Mason."

I gave him a small smile, and he walked away.

"Looks like you made a new friend." Hanna grinned as she grabbed my glass. "Refill?"

"Nah, I'm going to head home." I threw some cash down.

CHAPTER 24

$\mathcal{M}$ ason
      I had texted Sara on my way home to ask her if she wanted a burger from the place around the corner from the apartment. I was starving and a burger sounded good.

After I got home, I set the bag of food down on the island, grabbed a bottle of water from the fridge and went straight to my bedroom to change. I stopped in the doorway and smiled when I saw Sara lying across the bed completely naked.

"Hello there, beautiful." I quickly pulled my shirt over my head and tossed it to the floor.

"Hello yourself, handsome." She grinned.

"To what do I owe this surprise?" I kicked off my shoes and undid my pants.

"I'm horny." The corners of her mouth curved upward in a seductive smile.

"Good enough reason for me."

I pulled off my pants and underwear and climbed on the bed as I softly kissed her lips.

"If you want to eat first, go ahead. I can wait." She ran her finger down my chest.

"I'm going to eat, sweetheart, but it won't be that burger first." I gave her a wink as I made my way down her torso.

&.

I let out a loud moan as I exploded inside her. Trying to catch my breath, I pressed my lips against her bare shoulder.

"Have I satisfied your sexual need?" I asked.

"You always do." She smiled with the turn of her head.

I pulled out of her and she rolled on her back. Pulling the condom off, I disposed of it in trash and grabbed my bag of food from the kitchen counter.

"Fry?" I pulled one out and held it up to her.

"Thanks."

I climbed in next to her and sat up so I could eat.

"By the way, you reek of scotch," she spoke as she reached over and grabbed another fry.

"That's because I was at Rudy's. Are you working tomorrow?"

"No. It's my day off. Why?"

"Good. I invited someone over for dinner. You are more than welcome to join us. I'd like you to meet him."

"Okay. Who is this man I'll be meeting?"

"His name is Jack. I met him at Rudy's, and we sat and talked for a couple hours."

"What?" Her brows furrowed. "You just met a strange guy at the bar and now you invited him over for dinner?"

"I know. It sounds crazy and so out of character for me. But there's something about him."

"Like what?"

"I don't know. We connected. He was so easy to talk to and listen to. I know this sounds weird, but I kind of feel like I've known him my entire life."

"Sounds like you're in love." She grinned.

"Shut up." I laughed.

"Seriously, Mason. Don't you think it's kind of dangerous inviting a stranger to the apartment?"

"I do it—or at least I did it all the time."

"But those were women. Big difference. What if he's a murderer? What do you know about him?"

"He's not a murderer. He's from Alaska and he's a crab fisherman. Well, he used to be. He's retired now."

"So he's an Alaskan crab fisherman murderer?"

"Very funny." I nudged her shoulder.

"How old is this guy?"

"I'd say around sixty, maybe early sixties."

"Really?" She bit down on her bottom lip.

"Yeah. He just got into New York about a week ago and doesn't know anyone. We talked, he told me some stories, and I invited him over. I think you'll like him."

❧

Sara

I found it odd that Mason would just up and invite a total stranger to the apartment for dinner. But then again, he invited a total stranger to live with him. That stranger being me. He was a kind-hearted person, and his generosity made me fall more in love with him. But I still couldn't help the feeling that something wasn't right.

When we got back from the grocery store, I realized we forgot to pick up something, so Mason ran to the corner store to get it. As I was putting away the groceries, there was a knock on the door. When I opened it, Nathan stood there with a grin.

"Hello, Sara."

"Hey, Nathan. Come on in."

"Mason told me he'd be home in a few and just to wait for him."

"Yeah. He just ran to the corner store. We forgot something we need for dinner."

"Oh. So you two are cooking dinner together?" He smirked.

"Yeah. Mason invited this guy over he met last night at Rudy's."

"What guy?"

"Some guy named Jack. I guess he's from Alaska and was a crab fisherman. They got to talking last night over drinks and he invited him over."

"That's weird. That doesn't sound like my brother," he spoke.

"I thought that too, but then again, he did invite me to live with him."

"True." He chuckled. "I guess my little brother is changing."

"Who's changing?" Mason asked as he walked through the door.

"You are. Sara was just telling me how you invited some random guy from Rudy's over for dinner."

"Yeah. His name is Jack. I'll go get that shirt for you."

"When do I get to meet this new friend?" Nathan shouted.

"Dude, I just met the guy. I don't know." Mason walked over and handed him his shirt.

"Thanks, bro. Don't forget we're meeting at the gym tomorrow morning at six. Elijah said he has to be at the office by eight."

"I'll be there. See you later, bro."

While Mason seasoned the steaks, I started prepping the salad. As I was cutting up the cucumbers, the knife slipped and cut my finger.

"Shit!" I yelled as I grabbed hold of my finger and blood poured from it onto the counter.

"Here," Mason spoke as he grabbed a towel. "Wrap this tightly around it."

I couldn't help but smile at him.

"What?" The corners of his mouth curved upward.

"I am a doctor, you know."

"I know. Sorry. It's just the medical training side of me."

After a few moments, Mason took the towel and slowly unwrapped it so he could look at my finger.

"Good news, doctor. I don't think you need stitches. I'll go grab a butterfly from the bathroom and I'll have you fixed up in a flash." He winked.

I sighed as I looked at my finger. Within a moment, he was back, and he placed the butterfly Band-aid around my finger.

"All better. And for being such a star patient, I have a nice big, satisfying lollipop for you."

"I'll suck on it later. Your friend will be here in a few minutes." I gave him a wink as I walked away.

"Damn you, Sara."

I laughed all the way to my bedroom.

CHAPTER 25

*M*ason

"Jack, come on in," I spoke as I opened the door.

"Thanks, Mason. It's good to see you again."

"You too. Jack, this is my roommate, Sara. Sara, this is Jack."

"You neglected to tell me you lived with a beautiful woman. The pleasure is all mine, darling," he spoke as he brought Sara's hand up to his lips.

"It's nice to meet you, Jack. You two go sit down while I get dinner," Sara spoke.

"I can help," I said.

"No. No. You go sit and talk with your friend." She smiled.

We both sat down at the table and Jack leaned over.

"Roommates?"

"Yes. Just roommates. It's a long story." I smiled.

"And one I'm looking forward to hearing."

Sara put dinner on the table and took her seat. While we ate, Jack shared some of his fishing stories and how close he came to death multiple times over the years.

"Mason told me you don't have any family here," Sara spoke.

"No. I don't."

"What about back in Alaska?" she asked.

"Not really. I guess you could consider my crew part of my family. It's always been just me."

I could tell by the look on his face that it bothered him, and I wished Sara would stop asking him questions like that. Once we were finished eating, Sara got up from the table and took the plates to the kitchen sink.

"Let me help," Jack said as he got up. "It's the least I could do for the fine meal you cooked."

"Thanks, Jack, but that's not necessary. You sit down and relax. I've got this." She smiled.

He walked over to the sofa table where I had a picture of me, my mom and my brothers from her wedding in Vegas.

"Is this your family?" he asked as he picked up the frame and stared at the picture.

"Yeah. That's my mom and my brothers."

"Your mother is a beautiful woman if you don't mind me saying so."

"Not at all. She is beautiful. That was actually taken not too long ago at her wedding."

"What about your dad?" he asked.

"Never knew him. He took off right after I was born."

"I'm sorry to hear that. You never tried to look for him?"

"No. He was something we didn't discuss in our household. We all figured if he could walk out on his family the way he did, he wasn't worthy of knowing us."

He set the picture down and walked back over to the table.

"You have a beautiful family, Mason."

"Thanks."

"If you don't mind me asking, do your brothers have dangerous jobs as well?" he smirked.

"Elijah is a lawyer and Nathan is an airline pilot."

"Good careers. Your mother raised you boys well."

*S*ara

I stood at the sink and listened to every word Jack said. Something about him wasn't sitting right with me. Sure, he was a nice man, but something seemed off. I couldn't quite put my finger on it. When we were sitting at the table eating dessert, I noticed something. Something a doctor would notice, and I figured maybe that was the reason he came to New York.

"So, Jack, what brings you to New York?"

"No specific reason. I guess I just wanted to visit and catch some sights that everyone in the world talks about."

"Oh yeah. Like what?"

"Statue of Liberty, Empire State Building, museums. Things like that."

"I thought you said last night you came here for personal reasons," Mason said.

"I didn't really think you'd want to hear about that boring stuff." He smirked. "To me, those are personal reasons."

"Yeah. I guess," Mason said.

"How long do you plan on staying?" I asked.

"I'm not sure yet. Enough talk about me. What is it you do, Sara?"

I grabbed three beers from the fridge and took them over to the table.

"I'm a doctor."

"Really?" His brow raised. "Any kind of specialty?"

"ER."

"Good choice. Like Mason here, you also save lives. You two are a good fit for roommates." He gave us a wink. "Are you from New York?"

"No. I'm from Connecticut. I moved here to be closer to my mother. She's in a care facility for Alzheimer patients."

"Gee. I'm sorry to hear that."

"And your father?"

My heart started racing as I swallowed the lump in my throat.

"I don't have a father as far as I'm concerned, and we'll leave it at that."

"Okay. Got it. Thanks for the dinner and the beer. It was all very good. You two have made my stay here welcoming and I appreciate that. I better get going now."

He got up from the table and headed towards the door.

"Jack, I'll be at the station the next couple of days if you want to stop by. I'll give you a tour."

"I'd like that, Mason." He gave him a small smile. "You two enjoy the rest of your evening."

As soon as he walked out the door, Mason sat back down at the table.

"Well, what did you think?" he asked.

"Something is up with that guy."

"Oh, come on, Sara. He's a good man."

"You don't even know him, Mason."

"And neither do you to say that," he spoke with irritation as he collected the beer bottles from the table.

"Why are you giving me an attitude about it?"

"Because you're being rude. The guy was nothing but nice and polite, and instantly you think something is up with him."

"What is your fascination with this guy? For fuck's sake, you just met him twenty-four hours ago, and it's like he's your new best friend. You asked me my opinion, and I gave it to you. You didn't think it was odd how he was asking you about your family?"

"Not at all. He's a lonely man, and he's trying to get to know me. And to answer your question about my supposed 'fascination' with the guy, I find him interesting and easy to talk to," he spoke with an abrupt tone. "And by the way, jealousy isn't very flattering on you."

"Excuse me?" I placed my hand on my hip.

"The way you're behaving, you're acting like you're jealous of him or something."

"Really? That's what you think?" I spoke in anger.

"Yeah. It's exactly what I think," he shouted.

I put my hands up.

"Fine. Think whatever you want. I'm not discussing this any further. It's obvious if someone doesn't agree with you or see things the way you see it, they're automatically wrong. I'm going to my room."

"You're bat shit crazy, Sara," he shouted as I walked away.

"So I've been told." I rolled my eyes and slammed my bedroom door shut.

CHAPTER 26

*M*ason

"Dammit," I said as I gripped the counter and inhaled a deep breath.

Grabbing my keys, I headed towards the door. Placing my hand on the knob, I stopped, then turned around, threw my keys on the counter and headed straight to my bedroom. I had no idea what the fuck her problem was with Jack, but I wasn't having it. She had no right to judge him the way she did.

I got up from the bed, walked to her room and opened the door in an angry manner.

"Excuse me!" she shouted.

"You have no right to judge someone before you even get to know them." I pointed at her. "I thought you would have learned that already since you did the same thing with me."

She picked up a pillow from the bed and threw it at me, hitting me square in the face.

"Get out of my room!"

"Real mature, Sara. Just think about what I said." I shut the door.

This was ridiculous. Why was I even arguing about it with her? I didn't give two shits what she thought.

I got up early and headed to the gym to meet my brothers. When I walked in, I only saw Elijah sitting on the bench.

"Hey bro," I said. "Where's Nathan?"

"He's on his way. I guess Ruby was up all night with a fever."

"Oh shit. I hope she feels better today."

Just as I said that, Nathan walked over and joined us.

"How's Ruby?" I asked.

"She still has a fever of 102. Allison is going to call the doctor today and see if she can get her in."

"I know how worrisome it is when your child is sick. She'll be okay, bro," Elijah said as he patted Nathan's shoulder.

I grabbed two plates and started warming up.

"So, how was dinner last night with your new BFF." Nathan smirked.

"Who? What?" Elijah asked.

"Our little brother here has a new BFF. He met him at Rudy's a couple days ago and had him over for dinner last night."

"Shut up, douchebag." I shot him a look.

"Who is this guy?" Elijah asked.

"He's just a guy I met. He's a crab fisherman from Alaska."

"Damn. That's a pretty dangerous job," Elijah spoke as he did some bicep curls.

"He sat down next to me at Rudy's and we just started talking. He's an easy guy to talk to."

"How old is this guy?" Elijah asked.

"I don't know exactly, but I'd say sixty-ish."

"Damn, bro. He's older than Mom." Nathan laughed. "What are you doing, looking for a father figure?" He laughed.

As much as I wanted to punch him, I couldn't do it in the middle of the gym. Elijah raised his brow at me.

"He's a nice guy and I feel sorry for him because he's alone. He has no family and no friends from what I can tell. I was just being nice."

Nathan laid down on the bench and gripped the barbell.

"Bro, you really need to add some more weight. I can lift more than what you're lifting," I said.

"Then put another plate on," he said.

Elijah looked at me with furrowed brows, for he knew what I was about to do. I grabbed two forty-five-pound plates and put them on each side and stood behind to spot him.

"Come on, bro. You can do it."

He grunted as he struggled to lift it.

"Bro, I'm losing it," he said. "Grab it."

"Take back what you said about a father-figure, douchebag," I said as I stared down at him.

"What the fuck, dude! My arms are going to collapse."

"Take back what you said!"

"I take it back. I take it back!"

I grabbed the barbell and put it up. Nathan sat up, trying to catch his breath as he slowly shook his head at me.

"You wait, bro. You wait." He pointed his finger at me. "And you." He pointed at Elijah, who stood there with a smirk on his face. "You were just going to let me get hurt?"

"Hey, this is between you and him. I'm staying out of it."

We finished up our workout and left the gym.

"Are you working today?" Elijah asked me.

"Yeah. I need to be there in a couple hours."

"Maybe I'll swing by later and we can have lunch," he said as he placed his hand on my back.

"Sure. Sounds good."

By the time I got home, Sara had already left for work. I wouldn't be seeing her for the next couple of days, which was good. It would give us both time to cool down. After I showered, I repacked my bag and headed to the fire station.

I had just gotten back from a rescue and headed to my office to do some paperwork when Elijah came in.

"Do you have time to have lunch with your brother?" he asked as he stood in the doorway holding up a plastic bag.

"Hey, bro." I smiled as I got up and gave him a bro handshake.

"Yeah. I'm starving. What did you bring?" I asked as we walked to the kitchen.

"Subs from that deli you love by the office."

"Shit. Tell me you got me the Dagwood?"

"Of course." He smiled as he took it out of the bag.

"You're the best, bro."

Walking over to the refrigerator, I grabbed a couple bottles of water and set them down on the table.

"Tell me about this guy friend of yours."

"Is that why you wanted to have lunch?" I asked as I bit into my sub.

"No. It's been a while since just the two of us talked."

"Elijah, he's just a guy. I don't know why everyone is making a big fucking deal about it."

"Who is everyone besides Nathan?"

"Sara for one. We got into a fight last night."

"Over Jack?"

"Yeah. I asked her what she thought about him, and she said something is up with him. It was as if she doesn't trust him."

"So you got into a fight over her opinion?" His brow arched.

"Yeah. Because she shouldn't judge people she doesn't know. She only talked to him for a couple of hours and she already made her decision about him."

"Let me ask you something. Why do you care so much what Sara thinks about him? Is something going on between the two of you that you haven't told us about?"

Shit. If I lied to him, he'd know. He always knew when people were lying. It was the lawyer in him.

"We have an arrangement."

"What kind of arrangement?" His eye narrowed.

"Friends with benefits type of arrangement."

"You two are still sleeping together?"

"Yeah."

"That explains why you haven't been forthcoming with your one-night stands like you usually are." He smirked. "So how is it working out?"

"Great. She's just as horny as I am all the time. We have rules."

He sat across from me and slowly shook his head.

"You two and your rules. Anything else about her I should know about?" A smirk crossed his lips.

"If you're looking to get the answer that I'm madly in love and can't live without her, the answer is no. That is yours and Nathan's weakness, not mine. No offense. Don't get me wrong, I love Aspen and Allison to death, but you know where I stand as far as relationships are concerned."

"But you let some random stranger cause an argument between the two of you. If you didn't care about her, you wouldn't care what she thinks. Just saying." He brought the bottle of water up to his lips.

"It's the principle of the matter. He gave her no reason at all for her to feel the way she does."

"I will admit, I am concerned how you took to this guy so quickly."

"Come on, Elijah. Fuck."

Suddenly, the alarm went off, and a call came through about a shopping plaza fire.

"I have to go, bro. Duty calls," I spoke as I quickly got up.

CHAPTER 27

Sara

I loved my job, and I loved being a doctor, but I didn't feel complete or satisfied. There was a need deep down in my soul. A need that wasn't being met.

I was at the nurses' station doing some paperwork when Madeline, one of the nurses, walked over to me.

"Sara, Nathan Wolfe is in room six with his daughter. He's asking for you."

"Really? I'll be there in a second." I placed my pen in my pocket and headed to room six.

"Nathan, Ruby, what's going on?" I asked sympathetically as Ruby laid on the bed, not looking so well.

"Ruby was up all night with a fever and a sore throat. Allison called the doctor when she got to work this morning, but they couldn't get her in until tomorrow. I took her temperature again, and it was up to 103.9. There was no way in hell I was waiting until tomorrow, so I called Allison and told her I was bringing her here."

"You did the right thing." I smiled as I placed my hand on his shoulder. "Not feeling so good, are you, Ruby?"

She shook her head.

"Don't worry. We'll find out what's going on and get you feeling better." I smiled.

I raised the bed up, listened to her heart and chest, and then I checked her throat.

"Open wide, sweetheart."

After checking her throat, I reached into the cabinet and pulled out a strep kit.

"I'm going to swab the back of your throat. All you'll feel is a little tickle."

"I know. I'm used to this."

"Do you think it's strep?" Nathan asked.

"I do. Her tonsils are also inflamed. I'll send this down to the lab and order some blood work. Are you afraid of needles?" I asked her.

"No. But will you do it?"

"Of course, I will. I'll be right back." I patted her hand.

As soon as I walked out, Nathan came after me.

"Hey, Sara. How did it go last night with Jack? Mason was in a foul mood this morning."

"Not surprised. We got into an argument last night after Jack left."

"About what?"

"Jack. Mason asked me what I thought, and I basically told him I didn't trust him. He got pissed and told me I shouldn't judge people I don't know."

"Damn. Really?"

"I don't know, Nathan. Jack seems like a nice guy, but something isn't right, and I can't put my finger on it. I guess it's something Mason will have to figure out on his own." I grabbed the draw kit and headed back to the room to draw Ruby's blood. "You are an excellent patient, Miss Ruby." I smiled. "I'll walk this blood down to the lab personally and send a nurse in to give her some medication to get that fever down. I'll be back as soon as the results come in."

"Thanks, Sara," Nathan spoke.

"You're welcome." I gave him a smile.

On my way back from the lab, I got an urgent page from the ER.

Holding my stethoscope around my neck, I ran down the hall and straight to room three.

"What's happening in here?" I asked when I walked in.

My belly flipped when I saw Mason standing there, holding the hand of a very pregnant woman.

"She was already in labor when I pulled her out of the fire," Mason said.

"Please, doctor. My baby isn't due for another month and my husband is out of town on business," she cried.

"I need you to calm down and breathe for me." I placed my hand on her forehead. "I won't let anything happen to your baby. What is your name?"

"Katelynn."

"It's nice to meet you, Katelynn. I'm Dr. Davis." I gave her a small smile.

I reached over and grabbed a pair of gloves just as she let out a horrifying scream and the fetal monitor beeped erratically.

"Dr. Davis, the baby's heart rate is slowing," Corinne spoke.

"What's happening?!" Katelynn screamed.

"Call OB and get them down here now!" I told Corinne as I examined Katelynn and she was bleeding profusely.

I looked at Mason, and he knew it wasn't good as he stared at me.

"OB said it'll be at least twenty minutes," Corinne said. "They have an emergency upstairs."

"And we have an emergency down here!" I yelled. "She has placental abruption, and she needs an emergency c-section now. We can't wait any longer. Katelynn, I need you to listen to me. I have to get your baby out now. If I don't, your baby will die. Do you understand me?"

She nodded her head as the stream of tears flowed down her face.

"Please don't leave me," she said to Mason.

"I won't. I'll be right here." He gripped her hand.

"Get her prepped and call the neonatal unit."

A team of nurses ran in and we quickly prepped Katelynn for the c-section. I let out a deep breath as I lifted the baby out and a loud cry came from her.

"It's a girl." I handed the baby to Corinne.

Mason looked at me with a smile as I prepped Katelynn for closure.

"What's going on?" Dr. Carter, the OB resident, asked as he came running in while I was sewing Katelynn up.

"You're a little late."

"We had an emergency upstairs. You performed an emergency c-section down here?"

"I didn't have a choice. She had placental abruption, and the baby was losing oxygen fast. I had no time to get her upstairs."

"Are you even qualified?" he asked in a snotty tone.

"I'm more than qualified."

"I can take over," he spoke as he held out his hand.

"Step away from my patient, Dr. Carter. I will finish this and then you can take her upstairs."

"I'm reporting this, Dr. Davis. You'll be in serious trouble."

"Go ahead. I really don't care." I shot him a look. "The only thing I care about is that I saved that mother and her child."

As soon as I finished with Katelynn and they started to wheel her out of the room, she grabbed my hand.

"Thank you, Dr. Davis. Thank you for saving my baby."

"You're welcome. Congratulations." I smiled.

I removed my gown, and Mason followed me out into the hallway.

"You did amazing in there," he said. "I didn't know you could do surgery?"

"Long story." I rubbed the back of my neck. "You were really good with her."

"She needed me since her husband was out of town." He smirked. "Just another day on the job. We good?" he asked.

"We're good. By the way, your brother and Ruby are in room six." I gave him a small smile as I patted his chest and walked away.

Holding that scalpel in my hand brought back the feelings I'd missed so much.

CHAPTER 28

*M*ason

"Why?" I asked as she walked away from me.

I headed down to room six and when I walked in, Ruby's eye lit up. "Uncle Mason!"

"Hey, bro. What are you doing here?" Nathan asked.

"Hey, Ruby. Still not feeling well?" I asked as I kissed her forehead. "Hey, bro."

"No. But Sara is taking good care of me."

"Speaking of Sara. We haven't seen her in a long time," Nathan spoke with irritation. "I would like to know what's going on with Ruby."

"She just performed an emergency c-section on a pregnant woman I pulled out of a fire."

"Oh. Are the woman and child okay?"

"They're fine."

"I didn't know Sara could do that."

"I didn't either."

"Didn't know what?" Sara asked as she walked in the room.

"Congratulations on saving that baby, Dr. Davis." Nathan grinned.

"Thank you, Nathan. As for Ruby, she has a pretty bad case of strep throat. I'll prescribe some medication for her and order her to eat all the popsicles she wants." I gave her a wink.

"Yay!" I love popsicles.

"Thanks, Sara. I appreciate it," Nathan spoke as he gave me a hug.

"I better get going. I'm glad you're on the mend, Ruby." I gave her a high-five.

"Thanks, Uncle Mason."

"I'll see you later, bro. And I'll see you tomorrow night," I spoke to Sara.

*

J'd just gotten back to the station when Bobbie walked up to me.

"Hey, how is that pregnant woman?" he asked.

"Good. Sara had to do an emergency c-section in the ER. Something about a placental abruption."

"Oh wow. Is the baby okay?"

"Yeah. She seems to be doing fine," I spoke as I grabbed a bottle of water from the fridge.

"I forgot to tell you earlier. Some guy was here looking for you."

"Who was it?"

"Older guy. I told him you were with your brother and he said he'll come back another time."

"That's weird. I wonder why he didn't stay."

"I don't know, man. We're ordering chicken for lunch. Are you in?"

"Yeah. Get me the usual. I have a lot of paperwork to do and then we're going to do a drill."

"Gotcha, boss. I'll let you know when the food is here."

I took a seat at my desk and leaned back in my chair. Why would Jack leave like that? It would have been the perfect opportunity for him to meet Elijah. I didn't give it another thought and started my paperwork.

The next night after my shift ended, I grabbed my bag and headed home. The moment I walked through the door, my phone rang, and it was Nathan calling.

"Hey, bro," I answered as I gave a wave to Sara who was sitting on the couch.

"Hey. I just left Rudy's, and I met your friend, Jack."

"Really?"

"Yeah. He came up to me and asked if I was your brother. He said he recognized me from the picture you have of us from Mom's wedding. We got to talking and you're right, he seems like a nice guy."

"Good. I'm happy you think so."

"Anyway, I have to go. I'll talk to you later."

"Huh," I said as I placed my phone on the counter.

"What?" Sara asked.

"That was Nathan. He said he was at Rudy's and Jack was there and introduced himself to him. He said he recognized him from the picture. Nathan said he seems like a nice guy." I arched my brow at her.

"He is a nice guy. I just think there's something off about him." She smiled. "But we're good and we won't talk about Jack anymore."

"You're right. No more talk about Jack. I have a question for you," I said as I took off my shirt and starting walking toward my bedroom.

"What?"

"Do friends with benefits have makeup sex?"

"Hell yeah they do," she said as she jumped off the couch and followed me to my room.

CHAPTER 29

*S*ara
   He never disappointed. And this time, it was far better than I ever could have imagined. I wasn't sure if my body would recover, let alone my mind that was shattered by the feelings that intensified for him. I lay in his arms, his grip on me was tight as my head rested on him. My fingers stroked the flesh of his chest while the faint smell of fire still lingered on him.

   "You did an amazing job yesterday delivering that baby," he spoke.

   "Thank you."

   "I was watching the way you performed that C-section, and it looked to me like you were very skilled. Something I rarely see in an ER doctor."

   I lifted my head and sat up, gripping the sheet tightly that was against my naked body.

   "I was a surgical resident for three years and then it became too much when my mom's Alzheimer's progressed, so I switched to Emergency Medicine. The residency wasn't as long, and I needed to be there for her as much as I could."

   "So your goal all along was to be a surgeon?"

   "Yeah. My mom was a surgeon, and I wanted to be just like her.

She always told me I had what it took to be a magnificent surgeon, just like she was. When I was a kid, she'd sometimes let me watch her surgeries from the observation deck. She told me to watch carefully and learn as much as I could. I was always ahead of everyone else. I graduated high school by the time I was sixteen, graduated college in three years, and finished medical school a semester earlier than the rest of the students."

"Wow. I had no idea. You never mentioned that."

"It's not something I like to brag about. My mother did enough of that for me."

"Do you like being an ER doctor? I mean, truly like it," he asked.

"I do, but my heart lies in being a surgeon. Life is all about sacrifices and sometimes we have to make that one sacrifice that's the right choice at the given time."

He brought his hand up to me and softly stroked my cheek as he stared into my eyes.

"You're a good person, Sara Davis."

I gave him a small smile as I placed my hand on his.

"Would you like to come with me tomorrow and meet my mother?" I nervously asked.

"Yeah. I'd like that." The corners of his mouth curved upward.

*T*he next morning, we got up, got dressed and walked to Easton Gardens. When we stepped inside, Karen greeted us at the front desk.

"Good morning, Sara." She smiled.

"Good morning, Karen. Is she in her room?"

"Yes. She just got back from breakfast."

"Thanks."

I led Mason down the hallway, and when we approached her room, I stopped before opening the door.

"It's okay," Mason said as he gripped my shoulders. "I've been around Alzheimer patients before."

Opening the door, we stepped inside and I saw my mother sitting on the edge of the bed staring out the window.

"Hey, Mom," I said as I walked over and took hold of her hand.

"Who are you?" she asked as she stared at me.

"I'm Sara, your daughter."

"Sara." She smiled. "Look at how much you've grown. How are your classes going?"

I looked at Mason, and he gave me a sympathetic smile.

"They're going good, Mom. I brought someone I'd like you to meet. This is Mason, and he's a friend of mine."

She looked at him, and suddenly her eyes widened, and I could see the rage inside them.

"What are you doing here?" she screamed.

"Mom. Calm down," I said.

"I told you I never wanted to see you again, you filthy, lying, cheating bastard. How could you bring him here after what he's done to us?" she continued to scream. "How could you do this to me? I warned you what would happen if you tried to contact us again."

I looked at Mason in horror as Karen ran in and grabbed hold of my mother. I placed my hands on my head and walked out of the room as tears streamed down my face.

"Sara!"

I ran out the door to the courtyard, took a seat on the bench and placed my face in my hands. Mason sat down and hooked his arm around me, pulling me into him.

"I'm sorry," I spoke.

"You have nothing to apologize for. She doesn't know what she's saying. It's not your fault or hers."

"I should have known better. I just wanted you to meet her. I had no idea she'd go off like that."

"Can I ask who she thinks I am?"

I swallowed hard as I lifted my head and stared into his eyes.

"She thinks you're my father."

"Oh. What did he do to you, Sara?" he asked with seriousness.

I looked away and stared at the leaves on the tree that were blowing from the slight wind that swept across them. A part of me wanted to tell him because I wanted him to know me, all of me. But the other part of me was ashamed.

"Sara." He swept his thumb across my lips. "It's okay."

"My father gave me up and left when I was ten years old, when my mother found out he had another wife and child in California."

"What?" His brows furrowed.

"He was a computer engineer, and he traveled back and forth between the Connecticut office and the L.A. office. He was gone for a couple months at a time, sometimes longer. It was the norm in our family and how it always had been. Then one day, my mother received a call from his best friend. They had a bad falling out and that was his way of getting back at him. He told my mother everything. I remember the night she confronted him about it. I sat up against my door, hugging my knees as the tears fell down my face. There was so much screaming and name calling. The one thing about my mother was that she was strong. One of the strongest women I'd ever known, and she didn't put up with anything. She told him she was divorcing him and that he would never see me again. And if he tried, she would have him arrested for polygamy. He told her he would quietly walk away if she never told his other wife about us."

"Jesus Christ."

"He left that night without saying goodbye to me. And that is the reason I have issues trusting men. The night he walked out, he left a scar on my heart. I cried for weeks after that. My mother never shed a tear from what I saw. She buried herself deeper in her work and we were never to speak about it again."

He hooked his arm around me again and pulled me into him.

"I'm so sorry. I don't know what to say except you were better off without him in your life. Both of you were."

CHAPTER 30

Mason

Hearing her story reminded me of mine. I now understood the reason she didn't want to talk about him. There was an undeniable closeness between us. We shared a common bond. The bond of two people abandoned by their father. A key person who was supposed to always be there to protect their children.

"You and I have very similar circumstances, except my father left right after I was born."

She lifted her head and stared into my eyes.

"One day my mother came home, and he was gone. He'd left a note saying he couldn't do the father thing anymore, he wanted more out of life, and he was sorry. So I totally get how you feel and why you have trust issues."

"I'm sorry, Mason."

"Don't be. I'm not. I never knew the man and I never intend to."

"We're both pretty fucked up." She lightly smiled.

"We sure are." I kissed her forehead. "Let's get out of here and spend the day together forgetting about our loser fathers."

"Sounds like a good idea to me. What do you want to do?"

"First, we'll get something to eat, then maybe hit up a couple museums, and maybe take a ferry ride."

The smile on her face grew wide.

"It's a beautiful day out. What do you think about a picnic in Central Park?" she asked.

"Sounds like a great idea. Let's go picnic." I smiled as I kissed her forehead and we both got up from the bench.

We stopped by the apartment first and grabbed a blanket to take with us. Then we took a ride to a place called The Picnic Basket, where we grabbed a couple sandwiches, salads, veggies with hummus, baked sweet potato pieces and two lemonades.

"This was a great idea." I smiled at her as we sat on the blanket and ate lunch.

"I remember this one time when my dad—" She suddenly stopped and looked down.

I placed my finger under her chin and lifted it, so she was looking at me.

"It's okay. You have memories. To be honest, I don't know which situation is worse. You, knowing your father and then him leaving, or mine leaving before I even got the chance to know him at all."

"Both situations are equally worse. Our fathers are horrible people. At least yours left because he didn't want to be a father. Mine just started another family across the country while he was still married." Tears filled her eyes.

"Come here." I wrapped my arms around her. "Let's make a promise never to bring them up again. There's no looking back in the past, only looking forward." I pressed my lips against her head.

"Well, well. What's going on here?"

I looked up and saw Elijah and Aspen smiling at us.

"Hey, you two. Hi, pretty girl." I grinned as I kissed Mila, who was sitting in her stroller. "Shouldn't you be at work?" I asked as Sara and I stood up.

"We took the day off." Aspen grinned. "It's such a beautiful day, we decided we wanted to spend it with our daughter."

"Good for you," Sara said.

"You two stay here and talk. Us girls will take Mila to look at the flowers and have some girl time," Aspen spoke.

As soon as they walked away, Elijah sat down on the blanket.

"What the hell is going on?" he asked. "I walk up and find the two of you locked in an embrace, sitting on a blanket having a picnic."

"It's been a rough morning. Sara wanted me to meet her mother, so we went over to Easton Gardens and being the state she's in, she thought I was Sara's father."

"Shit. That's not good."

"No. Sara was so upset and ran out of the room. She finally told me what happened."

"And?" he asked as he picked up a sweet potato chip.

"Her father had another wife and child in California. I guess his best friend told her mother. She divorced him and said she'd keep quiet about it if he never contacted her or Sara again. He agreed and left without as so much as a goodbye."

"Damn. That's fucked up. How old was Sara when this happened?"

"Ten."

"Shit. She has something in common with this family."

"I told her about the man who left us. I somehow thought it would make her feel better."

"We all have to tell our story at some point, bro. You did the right thing."

"Yeah. Maybe." I looked down.

"It's okay, Mason."

"What's okay?" I looked up at him.

"To admit your feelings for her. I know it's hard, but the more you fight them, the harder things will be. Look at me and Aspen. If I was still fighting all my issues, we wouldn't be together and that would have been the biggest mistake of my life."

"I appreciate your words, Elijah, but I'm not you, and I'm not Nathan."

"Suit yourself." He got up from the blanket. "But if you want my opinion, I see the way she looks at you and it's not a friend with benefits look. Same goes for you." He pointed at me as the girls walked up.

119

"It was nice to see you, Sara." He kissed her cheek. "I'll talk to you later, bro. Enjoy the rest of your picnic."

"Bye bye." Mila smiled as she waved.

"Bye, baby girl. Uncle Mason loves you." I waved at her. "Take care, Aspen."

Sara sat down next to me and picked up a sweet potato chip.

"How about we pack up? There's somewhere I want to take you," I spoke.

"And where might that be?"

"You'll see. It's a surprise." I winked with a smile.

I had this overwhelming need to take her to one of my favorite places growing up. A place where I spent a lot of time as a kid. We left Central Park, dropped off the blanket back at the apartment, and then headed to SoHo.

"The New York City Fire Museum?" She smiled as I opened the door and we stepped inside.

"Yep." I grinned. "The history here is fascinating."

We walked around and I explained to her the history of fire-fighting while we looked at all the exhibitions, photos and memorabilia.

"Thanks for sharing part of your childhood with me." A grin crossed her lips as her beautiful eyes stared into mine.

"You're welcome." The corners of my mouth curved upward. "I hope you weren't too bored."

"Not at all. You were right. It's very fascinating."

After holding the door for her as we exited the museum, I tucked my hands in my pants pockets and she took it upon herself to wrap her arm around mine as we walked down the street. A feeling of warmth rose inside me. It felt right, and I liked it.

CHAPTER 31

TWO WEEKS LATER

*S*ara

I was happy in my little bubble with Mason, but I couldn't stop the feeling of wanting to talk to him about our "relationship." As much as I struggled with the fact that trust was an issue for me, I trusted him with all my heart. I'd never felt so alive as I did when we were together. I'd let my guard down and fell in love with him. The problem was, I didn't know if he felt the same way about me. I kept telling myself just to give it more time, but I wanted the security of knowing he was mine. We acted like a "couple" in every sense of the word. But it wasn't official until we had the talk. Just the thought of it terrified me. I was terrified of the rejection and the humiliation I'd feel if my love was unrequited.

Mason and Nathan had been spending more time with Jack. He still wasn't sure how long he was staying in New York, but I thought his newfound friendship with the boys would make him stay permanently. There was still a feeling inside me that something wasn't right with him. I didn't dare say anything to Mason about it anymore because I didn't want the strain on our relationship. Jack still hadn't met Elijah, which I found a little strange. Every time Mason would suggest the four of them going out for a drink, Jack would have some excuse as to why he couldn't.

It was a normal day in the ER, and I was standing at the nurses' station ordering some tests for the last patient I had just seen.

"Sara, they brought back a new patient in four. Male, age sixty, vomiting, severe abdominal pain and he looks a little jaundice."

"Thanks, Corinne."

I grabbed my stethoscope from the counter and placed it around my neck as I walked to room four. When I stepped inside, I stopped dead in my tracks when I saw Jack lying there.

"Jack? What's going on?"

"Sara. You work at this hospital?" He asked in shock.

"Yeah. I do. Tell me what's going on with you?"

"You know what," he got up, "I'm feeling better. I'm just going to go."

As he stood up, he doubled over in pain.

"Jack." I grabbed hold of his arm. "Get back in bed. The nurse told me you're vomiting and have severe abdominal pain. When did that start?"

"A few days ago, but it's getting worse," he nervously spoke.

"Okay. Just try to relax. I'm going to check your belly first."

He let out shrieks of pain as I pressed down on his tender abdomen. When I finished, I checked his eyes and the lymph nodes in his neck. They were swollen just like I suspected when he first came to our apartment for dinner that night.

"I'm ordering a CT scan and some bloodwork. Are you on any medications?"

He turned his head to the side and looked away from me.

"Jack? I am your doctor right now and I need to know if you're on any medication."

I watched as he swallowed hard before he rattled off a few medications he was taking.

"Those medications are used to treat Bi-polar disorder."

"Yeah." He looked at me with a sadness in his eyes.

"How long?" I asked as I took hold of his hand.

"Thirty years or so."

"Okay." I gave his hand a gentle squeeze. "I'm starting you on IV fluids, and as soon as I get your test results, I'll be back."

He gave me a nod, and as I was walking out of the room, he called my name.

"Sara?"

"Yeah." I turned around.

"I have pancreatic cancer."

My heart leapt into my throat when I heard him say that.

"What stage?"

"About two months ago I was in stage three."

"How long did they give you?" I asked.

"Six months. You can call Dr. Michael Shane at the Alaska Regional Hospital. He'll send over my records."

"Okay. I'll order your tests, and someone will be in shortly. Try to get some rest."

I had so many questions for him, but I needed to wait until his test results came back. Taking a seat at the nurses' station, I picked up the phone and made a call to Dr. Shane. Within the hour, Jack's medical reports came over the fax machine.

"Sara, Mr. Dawson's test results are in the computer," Corinne spoke.

"Thanks, Corinne."

After opening up his chart and reading the results, I went back to his room and shut the door.

"Well?" he said as he stared straight at me. "It spread, didn't it?"

"I'm afraid so, Jack. The cancer is in your liver. But you already knew that, didn't you?"

"I suspected."

"It also spread to your stomach and there's a few spots on your lungs, which puts in stage four. I'm so sorry."

"How long do I have now?" he asked.

"I'm not sure. Maybe three months, at best. I'm admitting you upstairs and the oncologist will be in to see you. Is that why you came to New York? For possible treatment options?"

"You know as well as I do, Sara, there's nothing they can do for me at this stage. I came here for other reasons."

"Were you ever going to tell Mason? He really likes you, and this is going to devastate him."

"This is doctor patient confidentiality and you can't tell him."

"Jack. You can't keep this from him." I furrowed my brows.

"I can do what I want. I will not cause them anymore pain than I already have," he shouted.

"What pain? What are you talking about?"

He looked away, and then it suddenly hit me.

"You're their father, aren't you?"

"I'm the man that helped create them. A father, I am not. I came to see how they were doing, to make peace with myself for walking out on them all those years ago. I never meant to get close to Mason."

"But you did, and then you met Nathan. Answer me this, Jack. Why haven't you bothered to meet Elijah? He's your son too."

"I've kept my eye on him and his family. I was afraid he'd recognize me. He was older when I left."

"He was four."

"And he was smart. One of the smartest kids I'd ever known. If anyone would put two and two together, it would be him."

"So what were your plans? Get to know them and then just take off without a word like before?"

"Like I said, I didn't plan on any of this. And as soon as I get out of here, I'm leaving New York. Mason and Nathan are never to know I'm here. Do you understand me? I know your career is important to you and I would hate for you to get fired or lose your medical license because you broke doctor patient confidentiality."

"Are you threatening me, Jack?"

"I don't want to, Sara. I like you. I really do, but this stays between me and you."

"Excuse me, Dr. Davis. I'm here to take the patient up to his room."

"Go head. We'll talk more about this later, Jack," I spoke as I arched my brow.

I let out a deep breath as I watched the transporter wheel Jack out.

I knew it. I knew something wasn't right with him. But I never dreamt in a million years that he was Mason's father. Shit.

Later that day, I received a text message from Aspen.

"Hey, Sara. Allison and Caitlin are coming over tonight, and we're baking cookies and drinking wine. We'd love for you to join us if you're not working. The guys are going to Rudy's tonight for a few drinks. Say around six-thirty?"

"I'd love to. Count me in. My shift ends at six, so I'll come right from work."

"Excellent. I'm also making tacos, so come hungry."

CHAPTER 32

*S*ara

"Sara." Elijah smiled as he opened the door. "Good to see you." He lightly kissed my cheek.

"Good to see you too, Elijah."

"The women are in the kitchen."

"Thanks." I gave him a smile.

As soon as I stepped into the kitchen, the aroma of tacos infiltrated my senses.

"Hello, darling." Caitlin grinned.

"Hi, Caitlin, Allison, Aspen." I gave a small wave.

"The tacos are just about ready. Go pour yourself a glass of wine and we can get this party started."

"Where's Ruby?" I asked Allison.

"She's spending a couple days at her grandparents' house."

"Ah, nice," I spoke as I brought the glass up to my lips.

As much as I loved and got along with the three of them, I felt like an odd duck with all of them being lawyers. What Jack told me weighed heavily on my mind, and Mason had every right to know who he truly was.

"I have a legal question for you ladies."

"Of course, darling. What is it?" Caitlin asked.

"I have this patient and he told me something personal about his family. I think his intentions are wrong and his family deserves to know what he told me. It has nothing to do with him medically or what I was treating him for. It was strictly of a personal nature. Does that still fall under doctor patient confidentiality?"

"It depends," Aspen said.

"Whatever this person told you, is it a threat to his family?" Allison asked.

"No. Not physically, at least."

"What that man told you, he told you while he was under your care. Doctor patient confidentiality rules still apply," Caitlin spoke.

"I figured. I just wanted to make sure." I sighed.

We each made our tacos and took a seat at the table.

"Where's Mila?" I asked.

"She's with my sister for the night. So I figured since she wasn't here and Ruby was with her grandparents, it would be a perfect night for all of us to get together and stay in and have a cozy girl's night." Aspen smiled.

"Of course, Nathan and Elijah weren't happy about it since there are no children around. Those selfish men wanted us all to themselves." Allison smirked.

"Pfft. They'll get over it, and I'm sure you'll more than make it up to them. I know I will even though my children are grown." Caitlin winked.

"Speaking of men." Allison spoke. "How are things going with Mason?"

"Good. He's a great roommate. He's clean, respectful, pays the bills on time, and he takes out the trash."

"And the sex?" Caitlin's brow raised and suddenly a sweat poured over me.

"Excuse me?"

"Sweetheart, it's okay. We already know the two of you are sleeping together." She gave me a smirk.

"How?"

"Well, you just confirmed it. It's a little trick we lawyers use to get the truth out of someone."

"Oh. Shit." I bit down on my bottom lip.

"Spill it, sister!" Aspen grinned.

"Yeah, come on, Sara. Don't hold back. We want details." Allison smiled.

I looked at Caitlin in embarrassment as she stared at me with an arch in her brow.

"There's nothing to be embarrassed about. I'm happy you're sleeping with my son. In fact, I knew it wouldn't be long before the two of you shacked up. My son can't keep his dick in his pants for anything."

I wanted to die. Even though she was the coolest woman I'd ever met, it still felt awkward talking about sex with her son in front of her.

"Please don't say anything to Mason. We have rules."

"Rules? Darling, what are these rules you speak of?"

"We have a friends with benefits relationship which consist of rules we put together. One of them being that we both agreed we would keep our relationship between us and not tell anyone."

"Please." Caitlin waved her hand in front of her face. "I've had many friends with benefits relationships in my time, and I wasn't ashamed at all about it."

"I'm not ashamed," I spoke.

"If the two of you are keeping it a secret, you're ashamed. So what, you have sex. Sex is a beautiful act and there's no reason you two should hide it." She grinned as she held up her glass of wine."

"And how is your 'friendship' working out?" Allison asked.

"It's great," I tried to sound as convincing as possible.

Aspen opened another bottle of wine and refilled our glasses. I could already feel the alcohol hitting me hard.

"It's okay if you've fallen in love with him," Aspen said. "We've been there." She pointed to herself and Allison. "We went down that scary road of love with the Wolfe men."

"I have trust issues," I spoke. "Major trust issues with men."

128

"Darling, nobody has more trust issues than I do or did. Trust me. If you love my son, tell him. Time and life are precious, and you can't let your past dictate your future. Believe me, I learned that the hard way."

"Yeah. What she said," Allison spoke.

"Honestly, I'm scared."

"Well, I have the perfect way to clear your head." Aspen grinned. "Come on ladies, let's dance."

She turned on some music and the four of us danced while we drank another bottle of wine. We moved around the living room, laughing and dancing the night away. I was drunk, and I didn't want the fun to stop.

CHAPTER 33

*M*ason

Nathan, Elijah and Tommy headed back to the penthouse, and I decided to join them and bring Sara home with me. Not to mention the fact that I wanted some cookies. As the elevator doors opened, loud music greeted us.

"What the hell?" Elijah said.

We walked into the living room and found the girls dancing and laughing.

"I do believe they're all wasted," Nathan spoke.

"Yeah. I think so." I laughed.

We followed Elijah into the kitchen to get some cookies, and there weren't any.

"Where are the cookies?" Tommy asked.

"Doesn't look like they got around to baking any," Nathan spoke.

Elijah walked into the living room and turned the music off.

"Oh, hey. We didn't hear you guys come in," Aspen slurred.

"Sweetheart, where are cookies?"

"Cookies?" She cocked her head. "Oops. We forgot to make them." She laughed.

I couldn't help but laugh as I walked over to Sara.

"Are you ready to go home? You're very drunk."

"I know. Don't tell anyone." She giggled. "I love your family." She wrapped her arms around my neck.

"I'm happy you love them. Let's go," I spoke as I removed her arms from my neck and hooked my arm around her to make sure she didn't fall on the way down to the cab.

When we reached our building, I helped her out of the cab and placed my arm around her as her head rested on my shoulder. Once we reached the apartment, I slid the key in the lock and opened the door.

"Come on, let's get you to bed," I spoke as I picked her up, carried her to my room, removed her clothes and dressed her in one of my NYFD t-shirts.

"Sex?" she asked as I pulled the covers over her.

"Not tonight. You're too drunk." I smiled as I kissed her forehead.

"You're no fun."

"Close your eyes and go to sleep."

"I love you, Mason," she spoke as she closed her eyes.

I stared at her for a moment as I swallowed the lump in my throat, while the beating of my heart picked up its pace. Stripping out of my clothes, I climbed into bed and turned the opposite way from her. Things just became very complicated.

֍

The next morning, I climbed out of bed and went for a run while she still slept. I couldn't stop thinking about what she said last night. Did she mean it? Alcohol always seemed to bring out the truth in people.

When I got home, I saw her sitting at the island gripping a cup of coffee between her hands.

"What are you doing up already? You don't have to be at the hospital for a few more hours."

"I wanted to nurse this hangover before I have to get ready. I can't be going to work and treating patients when I feel like shit. Ugh. Why did I drink so much?"

"I don't know. Why did you?" I asked as I took the carton of eggs out of the fridge.

"Aspen just kept pouring the wine, and it was so good." She took a sip of her coffee.

"Do you want any eggs?"

"No thanks. I think I'll go lay down for a while."

"Okay. Maybe you should do that in your room," I said.

"Um, Sure."

"It's just I'm going to take a shower, and I don't want to disturb you."

"Of course. I'll see you later."

She seemed to be acting normal. Maybe she didn't remember telling me she loved me. But she said it, and I couldn't forget it. The words kept replaying in my head over and over. I loved what we had. It was fun, and I was enjoying every second of it. But even good times had to come to an end at some point. I ate my eggs and then took a shower.

When I finished getting dressed, I walked to the kitchen and found Sara making a cup of coffee.

"I thought you were laying down."

"I couldn't sleep." She turned to me and seductively ran her finger down my chest. "I was thinking maybe something else would make me feel better." A smirk crossed her lips.

"Listen, Sara. Remember that rule we agreed to? The one where we should check in with each other periodically to see how things are going and if we have any concerns?"

"Yeah."

I inhaled a sharp breath.

"I think maybe we should take a break from our friends with benefits relationship."

"What? Why?" she asked in shock.

I knew this would upset her and maybe now wasn't the right time, but would there ever be a right time for this conversation?

"I just think things between us may have gotten a little out of control, and I think we both need to take a step back."

"Where is this coming from? I thought things were great between us."

"They are. It's just—"

"It's just you don't want to have sex with just me anymore, right?"

"No—that's"

She turned away as I could see the tears swelling in her eyes.

"Did something happen last night? Did I piss you off or something? Because I barely remember you bringing me home."

"No. Nothing happened. We just can't keep doing this. It's not healthy for either of us."

"Just all of a sudden you think that?"

"No. I've been thinking it for a while. I just didn't know how to tell you."

"Fine. Consider our friends with benefits relationship terminated. We'll go back to being just roommates. Now if you'll excuse me, I have to get ready for work."

"Sara, this has nothing to with you. It's me," I shouted as she walked away. "I need you to understand that."

She shut the door, and that was the end. I felt like a complete asshole. I hurt her and that's the last thing I wanted to do. I was stupid to think we could do this without any ramifications. I grabbed my key off the counter and left. Where was I going? I hadn't a clue. All I knew was I needed to get out of there.

CHAPTER 34

*S*ara

Tears streamed down my face as I sat down in the shower and let the hot water pour over me. I couldn't believe what just happened. Why the sudden change? Everything was perfect between us, at least for me it was perfect. Maybe for him, it wasn't. I would bet money he wanted to sleep with someone else but felt guilty if we were still having sex. I was a fool to think we could have a normal couple relationship. I let my guard down, even when I knew better, and it would be the last time I ever did that again. I finished my shower, dressed in a pair of scrubs and headed to the hospital.

I was still feeling the effects of the hangover and now I was nursing a broken heart. I felt shattered, just like I did when my father left. The hurt and pain of rejection stung, and I couldn't see how I would heal from this one. My last relationship, as much as he betrayed me, didn't hurt this bad. Probably because I was never in love with him. I used him as a way to learn to trust again. But with Mason, it came naturally. I didn't have to learn because it happened so easily. I felt like this was my punishment. A punishment cast down on me for being stupid to think that a guy could ever truly love me. My father didn't, my ex didn't, and Mason didn't. The best thing for me to do was to stay away from him and his family as much as possible.

It was my dinner break, so I went up to see Jack. I wanted to reassure him that he had nothing to worry about, but I also wanted answers. Answers maybe he had that would satisfy my need to know why my father chose his other family over us. I went up to his room and lightly knocked on the door.

"Come in."

"Jack, how are you feeling?" I asked as I stepped inside.

"Sara. I'm surprised you're here."

"I do work here, you know."

"You know what I mean. Have a seat if you want."

I walked over to where the chair sat next to his bed and sat down.

"You're looking better," I spoke.

"Better for a guy who's dying."

"I'm sorry, Jack. I know how hard this is for you."

"Nah. I've made my peace with the knowledge that I'm going to die, and now I've made my peace knowing that my sons are good, respectful and successful men who have their own families."

"All except Mason," I said.

"You can't fool me, Sara. I know what you two have been doing." He smirked.

"Yeah, but that's over now." I looked down. "Can I ask you something?"

"Sure."

"How could you just leave them like that?"

That was a question I'd been wanting to ask my father for years.

"I did what was best for them. For both Caitlin and the boys."

"You left them a note saying you didn't want to be a father anymore, and you wanted more out of life. How was that doing what was best for them?"

"I wasn't a good husband all the time and Caitlin would tell you that. I had a lot of problems and I did things I wasn't proud of. Shortly after I was diagnosed with bi-polar disorder, I left them. And I did it because I loved them, and it was the right thing to do."

"If you loved them so much, you would tell them who you are and what's going on. You will never make peace with yourself until you talk to them and explain your story."

"What happened between you and my son?" he asked.

"It doesn't matter. He cut it off. He doesn't want a relationship with me." Tears formed in my eyes. "Mason has a lot of issues because of you, and I have a lot of issues because of my father. He had another family that he chose over me, and that is something I will never forgive him for. But you still have a chance with your sons. You left because you were sick. Maybe you didn't go about it the right way, but you did what was best at that time."

"I'm sorry about your father."

"Don't be. It is what it is, and it set a pattern in my life."

Suddenly, my pager went off.

"The ER needs me. I have to go. Do what's right for your soul, Jack. Don't die with unfinished business."

I walked out of the room and headed down to the ER.

❧

*M*ason

I hadn't seen Sara in over a week. On my days off, and if she was home, she'd stay locked in her room. Her side of the refrigerator was empty, and she had stopped posting her work schedule on the refrigerator.

Another person I hadn't seen in a while was Jack. I went to the hotel where he stayed and the workers behind the desk told me he hadn't been there all week, but he didn't check out. I expressed my concern and the manager was kind enough to let me in the room as long as he stayed with me. All of Jack's belongings were there, including his suitcases, which led me to believe he was still in New York. Where the hell was he? I had tried to call him several times, but his phone went straight to voicemail. I took a cab over to Elijah's office to talk to him.

"Hey, bro. What brings you by?" He smiled as I stepped inside his office. "Hey, Mason." Aspen grinned.

"You know my friend, Jack?"

"Yeah."

"I think he's missing."

"What do you mean?" Aspen asked.

"I haven't heard from him in over a week. I keep trying to call, but his phone goes straight to voicemail. I went by his hotel room and all of his things are there, so he didn't leave town. I'm worried about him, Elijah."

"Did you ask Sara if he came into the ER?"

"Sara and I aren't speaking at the moment. But no, I didn't."

"Why not?" Aspen asked in a stern tone.

"We had a disagreement. I haven't seen her all week."

"A disagreement about what?" Aspen asked as she narrowed her eye at me.

"Sweetheart, it's really none of our business."

"The hell it isn't. Everything that goes on in this family is everybody's business." She walked over to me and pushed her finger into my chest. "Did you hurt her, Mason?"

"Aspen, please."

"Shut up, Elijah. I'm not talking to you. Answer me now, Mason Wolfe."

Shit. She wasn't playing around.

"It's complicated, Aspen."

"Complicated my ass. Everything with you Wolfe men is complicated. I know about your little arrangement."

"How the hell do you know about that?" I looked at Elijah and he slowly shook his head.

"We talked about it that night she was over. She didn't voluntarily tell us. Your mother dragged it out of her. In fact, we all suspected anyway, so we helped. You know, being lawyers and all, the poor girl didn't stand a chance but to tell us the truth."

"Fine." I threw my hands up in the air. "I told her our 'friend' relationship wasn't working out, and I ended it."

"A typical fucking Wolfe move. I am so disappointed in you." She shot me a look and left Elijah's office.

"Great. Now you've pissed her off and she'll take it out on me. Good going, bro."

"It's none of her business and it's none of this family's. I did what I had to do because she told me she loved me that night she was wasted."

His brow arched as he stood there with a smirk on his face.

"Hey, bro," Nathan spoke as he walked in. "Oh, hey, Mason. I didn't know you were here."

I sighed as I rolled my eyes.

"What are you doing here?" Elijah asked him.

"I just came to drop something off to Mom, and I thought I'd stop by and say hi. What's going on in here? I smell and feel some brotherly tension."

"Our little brother had a friends with benefits arrangement with Sara. She told him she loved him, and he called it quits," Elijah spoke. "Now they are not speaking to each other."

"Oh."

"Don't you say a damn word." I pointed at him. "Anyway, Jack is missing."

"What do you mean he's missing?"

"When was the last time you saw him?" I asked Nathan.

"About a week ago."

"Me too. He hasn't been seen or heard from since."

"Did he leave town?" Nathan asked.

"No. His stuff is still in his hotel room."

"That's strange. Talk to Tommy and file a missing person's report. He has connections."

"So do I," Elijah spoke as he shot Nathan a look.

"Anyway, back to Sara. Bro, you didn't tell me you had an arrangement and were sleeping together."

"I didn't want anyone to know because I didn't need shit from you."

"Ouch. That hurt." He placed his hand over his heart.

"Elijah." Our mother opened the door as she stared at the three of us. "Mason, I didn't know you were here. Anyway, I'm leaving for the day." Her voice was shaky, and she didn't look well.

"Mom, are you okay?" I asked.

"I'm fine. There's something I need to do. I'll be in touch." She shut the door and the three of us looked at each other.

"What the hell? Did you see the look on her face?" Nathan asked.

"Yeah. Something has her shaken," Elijah spoke.

"She said she's fine, so we'll just have to wait and see," I said. "I have to go. I'll talk to you two later."

"Wait," Nathan said. "I want to talk to you about Sara."

"Drop it, bro. I don't want to talk about her."

CHAPTER 35

*S*ara

It had been a tough week. I couldn't eat, I couldn't sleep, and most of all, I couldn't stand to be in that apartment. I picked up extra shifts just so I didn't have to be home when he was. This morning before I left, I packed a small bag so I could stay at the hospital since I had to be back tomorrow by six a.m. All of my co-workers knew something was wrong, but I didn't tell them what. Nobody knew about me and Mason and now wasn't the time to fill them in. After I discharged a patient, I pulled my phone from my pocket and saw I had a text message from Aspen.

"Hi. I just saw Mason, and he told me what happened. How are you? I'm so sorry. He's an asshole. We should talk. Let me know when you're available and we'll meet up somewhere."

"Thanks, Aspen. I'm not doing okay. I won't lie. I'm busy with work for the next few days, but I'll be in touch as soon as I have some time."

"Okay. You're my friend, Sara, regardless of what happened between you and Mason. Don't forget that."

"Thanks, friend."

Just as I placed my phone in my pocket and began walking down the hall, I saw Mason walking towards me. My heart raced beyond control.

"Sara."

"What do you want?" I asked as I continued walking.

"Have you seen, Jack? Has he been in here?"

I swallowed hard as I held a patient's chart tightly against my chest.

"No. And even if he was, I couldn't tell you that."

"He's missing. I haven't been able to get a hold of him in over a week."

"Maybe he left town."

"He didn't. I checked his hotel room, and all of his things are still there."

"I don't know what to tell you. I have patients to see."

His concern about not seeing Jack in a week over me was sickening and made me feel even worse.

"Sara." He lightly grabbed my arm. "I don't like this tension between us. We should talk."

I stopped, looked down at his hand and then diverted my eyes up to him.

"Do not touch me and there's nothing to talk about. You said everything you needed to that day. We're roommates, Mason. We don't need to say anything to each other. Just leave me alone." I walked away.

Tears filled my eyes as I stepped into the bathroom to compose myself before seeing my next patient.

🎀

Mason

"Fuck."

I was torn up inside. I honestly didn't think this would go on this long. I headed over to Rudy's and sat down at the bar. Just as Hanna set down my drink, I received a text message from my mother.

"You need to come to the townhouse now. We need to have a family meeting."

"I'm on my way."

I downed my drink and threw some cash on the bar.

"That's all you're having?" Hanna asked.

"Gotta run. My mother has summoned me."

"Good luck!" She smiled.

I walked up the steps to the townhouse just as Nathan pulled up in a cab.

"Bro, wait," he called out.

I stopped and looked at him.

"What do you think is going on?" he asked.

"I don't know, but I'm worried. Something is obviously wrong and to be honest, I can't take anything else right now."

"I'm sure everything is okay. It's probably just Mom overreacting about something." He hooked his arm around me.

When we opened the door, we saw my mother and Elijah in the living room.

"Hello, boys. I have your drinks ready for you." She held up two glasses of scotch.

I looked at Elijah as he sat on the couch with his drink in his hand.

"Mom, what is going on?" I asked.

Sit down. Both of you.

She took in a deep breath, and I could tell she was scared about something.

"Someone is here to see you and I want all of you to remain calm."

"Who is it, Mom?" Nathan asked.

"It's me, son," I heard a familiar voice from behind.

The three of us turned around and I couldn't believe my eyes.

"Jack? Oh my God, I've been looking for you," I said.

"Boys, this is Jack Dawson—"

"Our father," Elijah spoke through gritted teeth.

"What?!" Both Nathan and I exclaimed at the same time.

"Boys." Jack put his hands up. "I know how this must seem."

"Are you fucking kidding me?!" I shouted as I stood up.

"Mason, sit down and let him explain," my mother spoke.

"Let him explain?" Nathan scowled. "Explain what? We don't owe this asshole anything, let alone our time."

"He's right. Let's get the fuck out of here," Elijah said as he stood up. "I can't believe you," he shook his head at our mother.

"I said to sit your asses down!" she screamed. It was a scream and a tone I'd never heard come from her before. "I am your mother and you will do as I say, regardless of your age! Do you understand me!"

Shit. I thought she was going to pull out a wire hanger. That was exactly how she sounded. The three of us looked at her in shock and slowly sat back down. Jack walked over and took a seat in the chair across from us.

"First, I know this is a tremendous shock to you, and I wasn't planning on doing this. Confronting you, that is. But, after talking to Sara, she made a lot of sense."

"Sara? What the fuck does she have to do with this?" I scowled.

"I came into her ER last week because I'm sick. She admitted me and we talked."

I was pissed as hell she lied to me.

"What's wrong with you?" Nathan asked.

"Who the fuck cares," Elijah spoke as he finished his drink. When he went up to get another, my mother told him to sit down, and she brought the bottle of scotch to him.

"I'm dying. I don't want your sympathy and I don't want your pity."

"Don't worry. You're not getting any of it from us," I said.

"I know you hate me, and I don't blame you. I hate me."

"I doubt that very much," Elijah spoke.

"What are you dying from?" Nathan asked.

"I was diagnosed with stage three pancreatic cancer. I had surgery and then went through a few rounds of chemo, but it didn't stop the spreading into one of my lymph nodes. They gave me about six months to live. Now, I'm in stage four and the cancer has spread to my liver, stomach and lungs. I have about three months tops."

"Is that why you came here?" Elijah asked. "Because you're dying and you're looking for something from us?"

"I want nothing from you, Elijah. All I wanted was to see how well you all were doing."

"Now you've seen, so you can get the hell out of here!" Elijah spewed.

CHAPTER 36

$\mathcal{M}$ason
       I felt betrayed. Betrayed again by the man I despised the most. I befriended him, helped him, and this whole time, he never told me who he really was.

"Elijah's right. You can get the hell out of here now," I said.

"Boys, that's enough," my mother spoke.

"Really, Mom?" I narrowed my eye at her. "Have you forgotten what he did to you, to us? The pain he caused you for so many years. Your views on relationships which trickled down to us and the way we lived our lives."

"No. I haven't forgotten. But he is dying, and everyone is entitled to a dying wish, and his wish was to see how his sons grew into wonderful young men."

"How do we even know he's telling the truth?" Elijah said. "He could be lying because he wants something."

"I understand your lack of belief, son."

"Do not call me that!" Elijah shouted.

"You can ask Dr. Davis anything you want. She has all my medical records. And before you go off and get all pissy with her, Mason, I threatened her if she told you about who I was and what was wrong.

She couldn't tell you anything because of doctor patient confidentiality. Ask your mother and your brother. There's something else. I have another condition and it's been a real struggle and something I've had to fight against the past thirty years. I have bi-polar disorder. That is the reason I walked out on you. I left you boys and your mother, because I loved you. Leaving you was the best thing I could do, and I don't regret it at all."

"You're a sick bastard if you think what you did was right," Elijah spoke through gritted teeth. "Leaving your family and causing all kinds of pain."

"The pain you felt was nothing compared to what you would have felt if I had stayed."

"Did you know about this, Mother?" I asked.

"No." She shook her head. "He never told me he was sick."

"You must have had a clue at some point." Nathan yelled.

"Knowing what I do now, the things that happened and his behavior make more sense."

"The day I left, I went to Alaska, found a doctor there and got the help I needed. But it was hard to control, and it took many years before I could feel normal again. Your lives would have been ruined if I stayed, and that wasn't a chance I was willing to take. I knew your mother would take great care of you and make sure you were raised the right way. That was something I couldn't have promised."

"I'm not sitting here and listening to anymore of this," Elijah said as he stood up.

"Elijah," my mother spoke.

"No, Mother." He pointed his finger at her. "I've had enough. I remember that day you found his note. I remember it as if it were yesterday." He grabbed his suit coat and left.

"The last thing I wanted to do was cause you more pain," Jack spoke as he stared at me and Nathan.

"It's a little too late for that, don't you think?" Nathan spoke as he got up from the couch and walked over to our mother. "I love you, Mom, but I'm leaving," he spoke as he kissed her on the cheek.

"I guess I better get going too," Jack said as he rose from his chair.

"I've done enough damage to this family. Thank you, Caitlin, for giving me this chance to talk to them. Mason, you are one hell of a fine young man and I'm proud of you. I'm real happy I got the chance to know you." He gave me a slight nod and walked out the door.

I stared at my mother as she sighed, took a seat next to me and grabbed my hand.

"He needed to set himself free. Maybe we need to do the same."

I kissed her cheek and headed home. Stepping into the apartment, I headed straight to Sara's room. She was the one person I needed the most right now. Lightly knocking on her door, I slowly opened it to find she wasn't there. She should have been home by now. I went over to the hospital and asked Kylie, a nurse I've known for years, if Sara was still there.

"She's sleeping in the on-call room."

"Isn't her shift over?" I asked.

"Yeah. She said she's staying tonight because she has to be back here at six a.m."

"Thanks, Kylie."

Placing my hands in my pockets, I walked out of the ER. Since we'd been living together, she had never spent the night at the hospital. I guess she was doing anything she could to stay as far away from me as possible.

❧

I could barely get out of bed. Between Jack and Sara, I felt as if my life was spinning out of control and I didn't know how to stop it. I didn't have to be back to work until tomorrow, so I got dressed and headed over to the hotel to talk to Jack. Taking the elevator up to his room, I knocked on the door. There was no answer, so I went down to the lobby.

"May I help you?" the girl behind the desk asked.

"I'm looking for Jack Dawson. I just went up to his room, and he didn't answer."

"Mr. Dawson checked out early this morning. Are you Mason Wolfe?" she asked.

"Yes."

"Mr. Dawson left this for you in case you came by."

She handed me a white envelope with all of our names on it.

"Thank you."

I walked out of the hotel and down the street, holding the envelope in my hand. I didn't know what to do. Did I open it now or did I wait until I was with Nathan and Elijah? I grabbed a coffee and went to Central Park. As I sat on the bench with my coffee in one hand, I stared at the envelope in my other. Fuck it. I opened the envelope and took out the cream-colored folded paper.

Dear Sons,

I hope this letter finds its way to you, and if it does, that means I'll be gone when you're reading this. I know nothing I can say will erase the past and the hurt and betrayal that I've caused you boys and your mother. I told you why I had to leave all those years ago and I know you will never be able to understand. Being in the same room with the three of you last night was truly a dream come true for me. You have no idea how much I wanted to do that over the years but never had to the courage to face you after what I'd done. All I wanted was to see my boys fully grown as men, and I never intended to disrupt your lives. I hope that one day, you can find it in your hearts to forgive me. Not because I deserve to be forgiven, but for your own peace. I've lived the past thirty years unable to forgive myself for abandoning you, but after seeing you all and how you've grown into such fine young successful men, I can finally forgive myself for making the right decision, whether you believe it was the wrong one. I don't know where I'm going when I leave here, but wherever I end up, I know I will finally be at peace. I hope you will do the same to find peace in your hearts and put the past and me to rest. Whether you believe me or not, I love each and every one of you, just like I have since the day you were born. Take care of yourselves, your family and most of all, take care of your mother.

Love,

Jack

I sighed as I folded the paper and tears filled my eyes. Pulling out my phone, I sent a text message to Nathan.

"What time are you going to be home tonight?"

"My last flight gets in around six, so I should be home around eight. Why?"

"We need to meet at Mom's. Just head there after work."

"Why? We were just there last night."

"Jack is gone, and he left a letter. Just be there."

"Fine. I'll see you later."

I sent a text message to Elijah.

"Meet at Mom's tonight at eight o'clock."

"Why?"

"Jack is gone, and he left a letter."

"Good, and I don't care."

"For fuck's sakes, bro. Just fucking be there. I'll let Mom know we're coming."

"I'll see if I can be there. I'm not making any promises."

I sat there and shook my head as I dialed my mother.

"Hello, darling."

"Mom, we're all meeting at your house tonight at eight. Jack is gone, and he left a letter."

"I know." She sighed. "I'll see you then."

CHAPTER 37

*S*ara

I was sitting in the cafeteria having lunch when I looked up and saw Mason standing there.

"What are you doing here?" I asked with a sigh.

"I need to talk to you about Jack."

"Mason, I—"

"I know about him, Sara. I know he's my father and I know he's dying. He was at my mother's house last night and so were me and my brothers. I wanted to talk to you last night, but Kylie said you were sleeping in the on-call room and I didn't want to wake you."

"Sit down." I motioned.

"He told us everything. Now he's left town and left this letter for us." I slid the paper across the table.

She picked it up and read it.

"Why are you showing me this?"

"Because I think if it wasn't for you, he never would have revealed himself and he would have left town and we never would have known. And I want you to know that I'm not mad at you for not telling me. I understand why you couldn't."

"Really? Aw, that makes me feel better," she spoke with sarcasm.

"I'm happy he told you. Now if you'll excuse me, I have to get back down to the ER."

"How long are you going to stay pissed at me?" he asked.

"I'm not pissed at you, Mason. I'm hurt. Instead of telling me how you felt, you just out of the blue said I'm done with you." I got up from the table and walked away.

"I'm sorry about that. Maybe I did it the wrong way. Hell, is there even a right way? Because either way, I still would have hurt you."

"And that's on me," I said as I pushed the button to the elevator. "I let my guard down and I trusted you."

He grabbed hold of my arm, pulled me into one of the empty rooms and shut the door.

"What the hell are you doing?"

"I was up front with you from the start. In fact, we were both up front with each other. Then you told me you loved me, and it freaked me the fuck out. Not to mention that you fucking told my family about us and our arrangement."

"I didn't have a choice," I spoke through gritted teeth. "Your mother and sisters are all lawyers and they tricked me. When did I tell you I loved you?"

"That night after I brought you home."

"When I was drunk?" I laughed. "And you actually believed me?"

"People tend to tell the truth when alcohol is involved."

"Okay. So what? My bad. I thought we had something special, something different. But I was stupid to believe you could ever love me back."

"Sara, you're not stupid. You're one of the smartest people I know. It's just—" he rubbed the back of his neck.

"Don't Mason. Don't humiliate me than you already have."

I opened the door and walked out as I could feel the tears stinging my eyes.

"Sara, wait!" I heard him yell.

*A*fter my shift was over, I didn't want to go home, so I texted Aspen and asked her if I could come over. She told me to come and that she'd have the wine and cookie dough ready for when I got there.

"Hey, how are you?" She gave me a hug when I stepped off the elevator.

"I'm okay."

"Your face tells me otherwise." She smirked as she led me into the kitchen.

"Hey, Sara," Elijah spoke.

"Hi, Elijah."

"I'm glad you're here. I have a question for you. Jack said that you have all his medical records. Everything he said was true?"

"Unfortunately."

"So aside from his terminal cancer, he is bi-polar?"

"Yes. When he left New York and went to Alaska, he checked himself into a psychiatric facility for almost a year. He's been on a range of medication ever since."

"Thanks." He kissed my cheek. "I have to run. Apparently, he left town and a letter that I need to go read with my brothers."

"Mason stopped by the hospital today and showed me the letter. I'm sorry, Elijah. Maybe I shouldn't have talked him into telling you boys."

"You're a good person and you did the right thing. Is everything cool now between you and my brother?"

"No. Not at all."

He placed his hand on my shoulder. "He's battling his own demons just like me and Nathan did. Give him some time."

I gave him a small smile and a nod while he kissed Aspen goodbye and stepped onto the elevator.

"Come on, let's sit down. I was going to have us bake cookies, but I think maybe we should just eat the dough, have some wine and girl talk." Aspen smiled.

"Sounds like a plan," I spoke as I sat down.

CHAPTER 38

ONE WEEK LATER

*M*ason

The night we all met at our mother's and read the letter, was the night that we put our past to rest. Jack was gone and there was nothing we could do. Elijah had the hardest time coming to terms that he had walked back in our lives for a brief time, but he accepted it and we all agreed to move on. I thought the person who would take it the hardest would be my mother, but she was fine. She had Tommy to get her through it, Elijah had Aspen, and Nathan had Allison. I was left to deal with it alone, and I had no one to blame but myself. I was too scared to tell Sara how I felt about her, so instead, I pushed her away. It's what I'd always done. The only time I ever felt brave in life was when I was inside a burning building. But it was time for me to grow up and make things right between us. I missed her. I missed our relationship, her smile, the sex, and the way she'd steal my potato chips and lie about it after I'd find the empty bag in her room. I was in love with her and it was time I told her. I had realized I could no longer allow my past to control my future.

"Hey, you have a second?" she asked as she emerged from her room.

"Sure. I was just going to ask you the same thing."

"I just wanted to let you know that I'm moving out, but you don't have to worry about the rent because I will give you my half up front."

I swallowed hard as I stood there and listened to her.

"Sara, you don't have to move out. Where would you go?"

"California. I'm moving to California," she nervously spoke.

"What? Why?" My brows furrowed and my heart began to race.

"I'm pursuing my dream of becoming a surgeon, and I got offered a trauma fellowship at Cedars Sinai working under Dr. Grace Harper-Finn."

"What about your mother?" I asked as I stood there in disbelief.

"This is what my mother would have wanted me to do. A couple weeks ago, I visited her, and she told me how proud she was of me for becoming a trauma surgeon. That really hit me hard and I knew I wasn't living my life to my full potential and she wouldn't be proud of me for that. Anyway, I just wanted to let you know."

"When are you moving?"

"I'm leaving tomorrow. I'll send for my things once I get settled and find a place."

"Tomorrow? How long have you known about this?"

"A couple days. It all happened so fast."

"You quit your job?"

"I had no choice. My boss understood. He said it happens, and he wished me luck. Did you need to talk to me about something?"

"Um, actually I forgot what I wanted to ask you."

"Oh. Okay. If you remember, I'll be in my room finishing up packing." She began to walk away.

"Sara?"

"Yeah?" She turned around.

"I'm really happy for you. I know you'll be a great surgeon."

"Thanks, Mason." She gave me a small smile and went to her room.

I felt like I had been ripped apart inside. But most of all, for the first time in my life, I felt my heart break.

Three days later

I had been working the past couple of days and I'd made sure I wasn't home when she left. Probably a dick move on my part, but I already felt the pain of her leaving, and I couldn't bear to watch her walk out of the apartment with her luggage. I hadn't talked to my brothers at all about her moving to California. In fact, I hadn't talked to anyone in a couple of days except my friends at the station.

"Hello, darling." My mother smiled when I walked into the kitchen.

"Hey, Mom." I kissed her cheek.

After I said hi to the entire family, I went into the living room and poured myself a double scotch. This was the last place I wanted to be.

"Hey, bro," Nathan spoke as he hooked his arm around me. "I have great news."

"What is it?"

"The townhouse next to me just went up for sale and it's listed at a bargain price. It's perfect for you and you can afford it."

"Why is it listed at a bargain price?"

"Mr. Bentley passed away, god rest his alcoholic soul, and Mrs. Bentley decided the place was too big for just her and her six cats. So, she's looking to get rid of it quickly and priced it way below market value to get rid of it faster. Now, it needs some work, but what place doesn't. Anyway, I knew you'd love the idea, so my realtor is calling you tomorrow to set up a tour of the place."

"Nathan, come on."

"Come on, what?" Elijah asked as he walked into the room.

"I was just telling Mason here about the townhouse next to me."

"Great bargain, bro." He pointed at me. "You'd be stupid not to take it."

"You two do realize that I am in the middle of a lease, right?"

"No big deal. Sara is still living there. Just give her your half of the rent for the remainder of the lease," Nathan said.

"She moved out."

155

"What?" Elijah asked.

"She got a trauma fellowship at Cedars Sinai in California."

"Shit. I didn't see that one coming," Nathan said.

"When is she leaving for California?" Elijah asked.

"She left a couple days ago. Once she gets settled and finds a place, she'll send for the rest of her things." I threw back my drink and slammed my glass down on the bar.

"Bro, I'm sorry," Nathan said as he placed his hand on my shoulder. "But you have no one to blame but yourself. You fucked up in a big way and you did nothing to make it right."

"Do you love her?" Elijah asked.

I stared at him for a moment because I had never admitted to him or Nathan about how I felt.

"Yes. I'm madly in love with her, she's gone and there's nothing I can do about it."

"Boys, dinner is ready. Everyone in the dining room."

"Don't say a word about this. Do you understand me?" I pointed to both of them.

We took our seats in the dining room and as we were passing around the mashed potatoes, Nathan opened his big fucking mouth.

"Sara moved to California to do a trauma fellowship at Cedars Sinai. Our little brother over here won't tell her that he loves her and is feeling sorry for himself. Sorry bro, consider this an intervention." He shrugged his shoulders.

"Is this true, darling?" my mother asked.

"Yes!" I shouted.

"We will discuss this in private after we eat."

"There's nothing to discuss, Mother. This is her dream, and I'm not going to confess my feelings to her and try to hold her back. She's made her decision."

The rest of dinner was quiet, and I was going to kill Nathan the first chance I got. After we finished eating, I stood up, walked over to my mother and kissed her cheek.

"I need to get going. Thanks for dinner, Mom."

"You're not going anywhere. You are to go sit down in the living room and wait for me."

"Mom—"

She held up her finger.

"I said go sit down in the living room." Her voice was stern.

I sighed as I rolled my eyes, went into the living room and poured myself a drink.

"Did Dr. Sara really move to California?" Ruby asked as she sat down next to me.

"Yeah, Ruby. She did."

"I don't want her to move away. I like her." She pouted.

"I don't want her to move away either, kid."

"Ruby, darling. Can you go play with Mila for a while?"

"Sure, Grandma."

I sat there with a drink in my hand while Elijah and Nathan stood directly in front of me with their arms crossed and my mother sitting next to me.

"We're doing this because we love you, darling. You know this family sticks together."

"Mom's right, bro. We're doing this because we want you to be happy and if you don't try to get her back, you'll be one miserable prick," Nathan said.

"There is nothing I can do. Why can't you understand that? This is her life. It's always been a dream of hers to become a trauma surgeon."

"She can become a trauma surgeon here in New York," my mother spoke. "There's no reason for her to have to move to California to become one."

"If you would have told her from the beginning how you felt, she most likely wouldn't have moved across the damn country. She did it to get away from you," Elijah spoke. "You don't think it hurts her to the core that she told you she loved you and you flat our rejected her? And to make matters worse, you two live together and she has to see you all the damn time. You are nothing but a constant reminder of pain to her. I don't blame her one bit for moving away."

"Yeah, bro. Give her a reason to come back home," Nathan said. "You have to tell her how you feel about her."

"It's too late." I shook my head.

"It's never too late, darling. Our last name is Wolfe, and we don't stop until we get what we want. If you truly love that girl and you want her in your life, then you need to make it happen. You get your ass on a plane and go to California and bring her home. You tell her that she belongs here in New York with you and you don't hold anything back. I know it's scary, trust me. If I can do it, so can you. You are my son and I believe in you. The sooner the better."

I sat there and rubbed the back of my neck as I thought about her.

"Can you get me a private jet for tomorrow?"

"I'll make the call now." My mother grinned as she walked out of the room.

"I'm proud of you, bro," Elijah spoke.

"What if she says no?"

"She won't," Nathan said. "When two people are meant to be together, things have a way of working themselves out. And you and Sara are meant to be together."

"He's right, Mason," Elijah spoke. "Look at our family and how things worked out for me and Nathan. Aspen and Allison were put in our path for us to love them for life, and Sara is no different, and you damn well knew it when you let her move in with you."

"Damn, bro. That was deep," Nathan said as he placed his hand on Elijah's shoulder.

"The jet will be waiting for you at the airport tomorrow morning at eight a.m." my mother spoke as she walked into the room.

"Then I better go because I have some calls to make and I have to pack a bag."

"Good luck, little brother," Elijah said as he gave me a hug.

"Yeah. Good luck, bro. I know you'll do good." Nathan gave me a wink.

I stopped at the station on my way home to talk to my chief and rearrange my schedule.

"How long do you need?" he asked.

"Honestly, I don't know. I'd say a week to be safe."

He sat there and slowly nodded his head.

"Okay, Captain. I have approved your time off. I'll cover the next couple shifts for you and I'll get the rest covered. Go get Sara and bring her home." He smiled.

"Thanks, Chief. I owe you big time."

"You're right. You do, and I will be calling on that favor one of these days." He winked.

"Anytime, Chief. Anytime." The corners of my mouth curved upward.

CHAPTER 39

$\mathcal{S}$ ara
     California would be the start of a new life for me. After meeting with Dr. Grace Harper-Finn, I knew I'd made the right decision to accept the fellowship. Even though I didn't want to leave New York, I knew I didn't have a choice. I needed to make a fresh start, somewhere out of New York, out of that apartment and away from Mason. This was the perfect opportunity for me, and it couldn't have come at a better time.

The next morning, I got up early and started apartment hunting before I had to be at the hospital. I found two places I liked, and both had immediate occupancy. Now, I just had to decide on which one I liked best.

I was standing in the E.R. talking to Grace and her husband, Jamieson, when I heard someone call my name. Turning around, I stood there in shock and disbelief when I saw Mason standing there. Instantly, my heart rate picked up its pace, and a sick feeling took over me.

"Mason, what are you doing here?"

"Sara, you don't belong here. You belong back in New York with me. I love you and I want you to come home."

It mortified me that he did that in the middle of the ER. I looked over at Grace and Jamieson as they stood there with smiles on their faces.

"That man has balls. I like him," Jamieson spoke.

"Go on, Sara. Talk to him. It's okay."

"I'm so sorry. Oh, my God. I'm so sorry."

"Don't be. I think it's sweet." Grace gave me a wink.

I walked over to him, grabbed his arm and dragged him out the doors of the ER.

"Mason, for the love of God, what do you think you're doing?"

"We need to talk, Sara. Somewhere private."

"You could have just called me!" I spoke through gritted teeth.

"No. I didn't want to talk over the phone."

"So you flew all the way out here?"

"Yes, I did. I flew out here for you. Please hear me out."

"I'm in the middle of work. Come to my hotel room around eight o'clock. I'm staying at the Sofitel Hotel, Room 240."

"Okay. Thank you." He placed his hand on my cheek.

I walked away as my heart pounded. I was shaking, and I needed to sit down, so I went into the doctor's lounge and took a seat.

"I saw you walk in here, are you okay?" Grace asked.

"I don't know."

"Who is he?" She smiled as she sat down next to me.

I told her all about him and our friendship we had back in New York. After my shift was over, I headed to the hotel and changed my clothes before Mason arrived. My nerves were getting the best of me and I couldn't seem to calm down, so I did a shot of whiskey before there was a knock at the door.

"Hey." I opened the door as the sick feeling in the pit of my belly erupted.

"Hi." The corners of his mouth slightly curved upward as he stood there with his hands tucked into his pants pockets.

"Come in," I gestured.

"Thanks. How is the fellowship going so far?"

"It's great. I'm loving it." I sat down on the edge of the bed while he paced back and forth.

"Sara, listen, I'm sorry about us. I'm sorry for the things I said and didn't say to you."

"Mason—"

"Let me finish." He knelt down in front of me and grabbed both my hands with his. "I should have told you how I felt instead of pushing you away, but I was terrified."

"So was I. Do you know how hard it was for me to open my heart to you? I told you about my father. I have never told anyone that before."

"I know, sweetheart, and I love you. I should have told you that day instead of cutting off our relationship. I've been in love with you since the moment I laid eyes on you. I just wouldn't admit it because I couldn't. I miss you so much, and I miss what we had. Even though we said it was a friends with benefits relationship, we both knew it was more than that. You knew it, I knew it, hell, my family even knew it. I used to pride myself on being this awesome bachelor and not getting involved with anyone like Elijah and Nathan. But all that went out the window the day you moved in with me. It felt right being with you and when you're not around, I feel it deep in my soul. I feel empty inside. I never allowed myself to get involved with someone, and now I know why. I would love to blame it all on my daddy and mommy issues, but the truth is, I was waiting for you the entire time. No one has ever made me feel the way you do."

Tears filled my eyes as I listened to every word he spoke.

"You are the best thing that has ever happened to me and I would give up everything to be with you. I want your problems to be my problems. I want to hold you in my arms at night before we fall asleep, and I want to wake up to you every morning, to your smile and to your lips. You told me that your father left a scar on your heart. I want to be the one to take that scar away and make your heart whole again. I want you to be able to trust, and I want you to trust me because I promise that I will never hurt you again. I love you, Sara, and I want you to come back home with me for good."

Uncontrollable tears streamed down my face as he brought his hand up and gently wiped them away.

"I can't, Mason. I'm sorry. This is where I need to be and I'm staying. I'm sorry you came all this way. I just can't. My mind is already made up."

He slowly nodded his head as he brought my hands up to his lips and tears streamed down his face.

"I understand. You have to do what's best for you." He let go of my hands and stood up.

"Good luck to you, Sara. I wish you the best, and I will never forget what we had." He turned and headed for the door.

"I'm so sorry, Mason."

The moment he walked out the door, I jumped up from the bed and ran to it as I pressed my hand against the door.

"Mason," I whispered, and I lost it.

I didn't think I had ever cried so hard in my life. I crawled into bed, curled into a fetal position and sobbed until I could barely breathe. The stabbing pain in my heart was unbearable, but I had no choice. I'd made a decision, and I needed to follow through. This was my future, and I knew this wouldn't let me down.

CHAPTER 40

$\mathcal{M}$ason

I left California that same night a broken man. When I got home, I locked myself in my apartment and drank. I called Elijah and Nathan and told them I was on my way home alone and I didn't want to be bothered. They extended their sympathies and respected my wishes until the fourth day when there was an obnoxious pounding on my door.

"Open up, bro. Enough is enough," Nathan said.

"Yeah. Open up, little brother." I heard Elijah's voice.

Stumbling out of bed, I opened the door and turned away.

"Damn, you look like shit," Nathan said.

"When was the last time you showered?" Elijah asked.

"What do you guys want? I told you I didn't want to be bothered."

"Well, you can thank us because Mom was on her way over here and we stopped her, so you're welcome," Nathan said.

Elijah walked over to the Keurig and made me a cup of coffee while Nathan grabbed a garbage bag and threw all the empty scotch bottles and pizza boxes away.

"Drink up." He handed me my coffee. "We're not here to lecture you or anything. We're here to check up on you and make sure you're okay."

"Which we can clearly see you're not," Nathan said.

"I poured my heart and soul to her and she didn't care."

"It's not that she didn't care," Elijah said.

"Did she cry?" Nathan asked.

"Yes, she cried."

"Then she cared, bro. I'm sure this is hurting her just as bad, but she made her decision and that decision is her career. Do you honestly blame her after everything that happened here?"

"I know it's hard." Elijah placed his hand on my back. "But you have to pick yourself up and move on."

"You don't have a clue how I'm feeling. Neither one of you does. You both got your girls and your happily ever after. That was something I never believed in or wanted, and now that I do, it's so far out of my reach."

"There will be other women," Nathan said, and Elijah smacked his arm.

"What if I would have said that to you about Allison?"

"Right. Sorry, bro."

"Listen, I appreciate you coming by, but I really want to be alone. Tell Mom I'm fine, and I'll call her soon."

"Okay, little brother. We will." Elijah hugged me. "Clean yourself up."

"Take care, bro." Nathan hugged me. "You know we're just a phone call away."

"I know."

❧

One Week Later

I went back to work a couple days earlier than I said and immersed myself in it. I spent most nights at the station because staying in that apartment was too hard. Everywhere I looked

165

reminded me of her. Fires were breaking out everywhere, and I was grateful, for it kept me focused and it kept Sara out of my head, at least until we put the fires out.

I called Nathan's realtor to see if the townhouse was still available, and unfortunately it had sold. I needed to do something because I couldn't stay in the apartment anymore. I had wished Sara would arrange to have her things moved out because knowing some of it was still there, hurt even more.

As I was sitting at my desk going over an arson report, my phone rang, and it was my mother calling.

"Hi, Mom."

"Hello, darling. Don't forget family dinner is tomorrow and you will be there."

"Yeah. I'll be there. Don't worry. Today's my last day for the next three days."

"Okay. I'll see you later. I love you."

"I love you too, Mom."

CHAPTER 41

*S*ara

I was loving my job so far, but I was still hurting. Would this ever stop? I asked myself that every day. Every night when I closed my eyes, I would replay the night Mason was here, in my hotel room, professing his love to me. Instead of lessening, the ache in my heart grew stronger every day.

"Hey, Sara?"

"Yeah, Grace?"

"Jamieson and I would love to have you over for dinner tonight. What do you say?"

"Thank you. I would love to."

"Great. We'll see you around seven o'clock. I'll text you my address."

"Okay. I'll see you then."

On my way to the Finn's, I stopped at the store and picked up a bottle of wine.

"Hi, Sara. Welcome to Casa Finn." Jamieson smiled as he opened the door.

"Thank you. I brought some wine."

He took the bottle and looked at it.

"You have excellent taste in wine."

"Thanks. That was always my mother's favorite."

"How is your mother doing?" he asked.

"Pretty much the same. They let me Facetime her everyday so I can see her."

"That's great. Come in the dining room. Grace is just finishing up with dinner."

"I thought I heard you. Welcome to our home." She smiled as she set a dish of chicken on the table. "I had the nanny take the kids out for dinner so us adults could talk in peace."

After we finished eating, Grace poured me another glass of wine and placed her hand on mine.

"Go home, Sara."

"What?" I asked in confusion.

"Go home to New York. You belong there with him. Not here." She gave me a sympathetic smile.

"No, Grace. I can't."

"Yes, you can. I see how bad you're hurting. You think you're doing a good job of hiding it, but you're not. You're not doing yourself any good by denying what is meant to be. You love him so much, Sara. Go back to him. It's not too late."

"Grace, I—"

Just then her phone rang with a Facetime call.

"Hello, Richard."

"Hello, Grace. Everything good over there?"

"Everything is great. I have Sara here with me."

"Excellent. I would like to speak with her."

I sat there in confusion, for I didn't know what the hell was going on when she handed me the phone.

"Dr. Sara Davis, it's finally nice to meet you. I've heard a lot about you. I'm Doctor Richard Howell, head trauma surgeon over at Lenox Hill Hospital in Manhattan."

"Hi, Dr. Howell."

"Grace told me all about you and how excellent your surgical skills are. She sent over your credentials, and after reviewing them, you're exactly what Lenox Hill Hospital needs right now. I have a trauma fellowship position available and I'm holding it for you if you're interested."

I looked over at Grace, who had a big smile on her face. "Go home." She mouthed.

"Yes, Dr. Howell. I'm interested. I'm definitely interested."

"Excellent. I'll give you time to get back to New York and get settled. Your fellowship will start one week from today. Is that enough time?"

"More than enough time. Thank you. Thank you so much."

"You're welcome. I look forward to having you here with us. Enjoy the rest of your night."

"You too, Dr. Howell. I'll see you next week."

"Bye, Richard," Grace said as she ended the call.

"I don't know how—"

"You don't need to say anything. I know being a trauma surgeon is your dream, and your dream of both trauma and love awaits you in New York."

"Thank you so much." I hugged her.

"You're welcome. Just promise me you'll keep in touch."

"I will. I definitely will."

"We had you over for dinner because one, we like you, and two, we wanted to do this for you outside of the hospital. Plus, we know we won't see you after tonight for a long time. When you get back to the hotel, make sure you pack because your flight leaves tomorrow morning at six thirty a.m. with a two-hour layover in Detroit and arriving in New York at five-thirty p.m."

"Sorry about that," Jamieson spoke. "It was the only flight with the best option that would get you into New York early. For some reason, the airlines didn't offer any direct flights."

"You two are amazing people. Please let me pay you for the ticket."

"Absolutely not," Jamieson said. "It's our gift to you. Consider it a congratulations gift."

"Congratulations?" I smiled.

"On the new fellowship and reuniting with the love of your life."

I looked down as a thought entered my head.

"What's wrong, Sara?" Grace asked.

"What if Mason moved on?"

"Oh, sweetie. I doubt it. From what you told me, he loves you more than life and he's just not going to get over it that quickly."

I thanked them both again and headed to the hotel. I couldn't believe I was going home tomorrow. I'd just hoped Mason would be happy to see me.

﹩

While I was in the Detroit Airport waiting for my next flight, I found a Starbucks and grabbed a coffee. I wasn't paying attention to my surroundings as I took my coffee from the counter and quickly turned around, bumping into someone and almost spilling the contents of my cup on them.

"Oh, excuse—Nathan?" I stood there in shock as I looked up.

"Sara? What the hell?" He hugged me. "What are you doing in Detroit?"

"I'm coming home, Nathan."

"What? Are you serious?"

"Yes. Please don't tell anyone. How is Mason?"

"Let me grab a cup of coffee and we'll go sit down and talk."

He ordered his coffee, and as soon as it was ready, we took a seat on a bench nearby.

"I can't believe you're here. Are you on flight 315?"

"Yes."

"That's the plane I'm flying back to New York." He smiled.

"Wow. I can't believe this. I can't believe I'm talking to you, here, in Detroit."

"Fate, Sara. Fate. I was never a believer in that until I met Allison."

I couldn't help but laugh.

"To answer your question about Mason, he's a total hot mess. I've never seen him like that before and I don't ever want to again. Why the sudden change of mind?"

"Because I can't get over him. I love him too much, Nathan. And Grace, the trauma surgeon I was working under, knew it. So, she told me to go home."

"That was nice of her. What about your fellowship?"

"I start next week at Lenox Hill Hospital under Dr. Richard Howell."

"Excellent." He grinned.

"Do you know if Mason is at the station tonight?"

"He's off and tonight is family dinner, so he'll be at our mother's. I'm going there straight from the airport so we can ride together, and you can surprise everyone."

"Okay. I'd like that." I smiled.

"Man, Mason will be so happy when he sees you. He's been such a miserable douchebag." He smirked.

"I love him so much, Nathan."

"I know you do, love. He loves you too." He grabbed my hand and gave it a gentle squeeze.

CHAPTER 42

M ason
"Where the hell is Nathan? I'm starving," I said as I took a seat at the table.

"He just called, and he's stuck in traffic. He'll be here soon."

"Mom, can we just eat already?"

"Fine. Nathan can eat when he gets here. Dig in everyone."

A few moments later, the front door opened, and Nathan walked into the dining room.

"You already started eating without me?"

"Bro, we couldn't wait anymore. What the fuck took you so long?" I asked.

"Traffic, douchebag. Tons of traffic. There's a package for you on the front porch with your name on it."

"That's weird. I didn't order anything. You couldn't have brought it in?"

"Nah. It's not for me." He smirked.

"I'll get it after dinner."

"You better go get it now. It's pretty big and someone may steal it. You never know around here."

"Nathan! How dare you insinuate my neighborhood is bad."

"Relax, Mom."

I sighed as I got up from my chair and opened the front door.

"Sara?" I stood there in shock as my heart rate rapidly increased.

"Hi, Mason." A beautiful smile crossed her lips.

"What are you doing here? Is everything okay? Is your mom okay?"

"My mom is fine. I came home because I love you and this is where I need to be and where I'm meant to be."

I looked down, and when I noticed her suitcases, tears filled my eyes.

"You're home? For good?"

"If you'll have me."

"Oh my God." I threw my arms around her and pulled her into a tight embrace. "I love you so much and I missed you."

"I missed you too. I'll explain everything later."

I broke our embrace, placed my hands on each side of her face and kissed her soft lips.

"Mason, what is going—Sara!" My mother exclaimed.

"She came back home, Mom. She's here to stay."

"Thank the lord! It's so good to see you, darling." She hugged Sara tight.

"It's good to see you too, Caitlin."

Everyone walked into the foyer, and excitement filled the room when they saw Sara.

"Aren't you happy I forced you to go get your package?" Nathan smirked.

"You brought her here?"

"She was on my flight from Detroit. Imagine my surprise when I saw her in the airport."

"Douchebag." I smacked him. "Why didn't you call me?"

"And ruin the surprise? Never. I'm happy she's back, bro."

"Me too. I still can't believe it."

After everyone welcomed her back, I took hold of her hands.

"Are you hungry?"

"I am. But not for food," she whispered in my ear and instantly my cock started to spasm.

SANDI LYNN

"Hey, Mom, I'm taking Sara home."

"Darling, don't you want to stay and eat?" she asked her.

"Mom, please. We need to go home."

"Oh. Right. You two have a lot of catching up to do. Have fun and don't hurt yourselves." She gave us a wink.

I grabbed her luggage and threw them in the trunk of the cab. She climbed in first, and I slid next to her and wrapped my arm around her while she laid her head on my shoulder.

"I still can't believe you're here," I said. "What about your fellowship?"

"I start a new one next week at Lenox Hill Hospital."

"Really? That's great. We bring more victims there than at your last hospital. I'll be seeing you all the time." I smiled as I kissed the top of her head.

The cab couldn't get to our apartment building fast enough. As soon as we reached the apartment, I unlocked the door and rolled the suitcases inside. I wasted no time smashing my mouth against hers, picking her up and carrying her straight to the bedroom.

"I have missed your lips so much," I spoke as I broke our kiss and pulled my shirt over my head.

"I missed everything about you." She unbuckled my belt.

"Oh baby, you have no idea what I'm going to do to you tonight." I took down my pants.

"You can do anything you want as long as you never let me go." She pulled off her shirt and bra and laid down on the bed.

I climbed on the bed and hovered over her, tracing her beautiful breasts with my fingers.

"I will never let you go again." I leaned down and softly brought my lips to hers.

The way we made love was unlike anything I'd ever experienced. It was as if our bodies met each other for the first time. We didn't need words, only the subtle sound of her breath, the beating of her heart and the soft moans that escaped her lips told me everything I wanted to hear. She whispered in my ear she didn't want to use condoms anymore and I granted her wish. I pushed into her inch by inch and

174

the warmth inside her took me in. The magical feeling of skin to skin intoxicated me. Her nails dug into the flesh of my back while hers arched as she orgasmed. I leaned in and whispered in her ear, "I love you" as she tightened around my cock, causing me to explode inside her. My body fell upon hers as I tried to catch my breath. Her grip around me tightened, assuring me she was never letting go. Before rolling off her, I lifted my head and kissed her lips.

We lay there, our bodies tangled together as I stroked her soft hair.

"Do you work tomorrow?" she asked.

"No. I have the next two days off and we are not leaving this bed."

"I love the sound of that. Do you promise?"

"I promise you the world, baby." I kissed the top of her head.

❧

The next morning, I got up and went into the kitchen to make us each a cup of coffee.

"Your phone is ringing, and it's your Mom," Sara yelled from the bedroom.

"Answer it."

Before the second cup of coffee finished brewing, Sara walked over and kissed me on the lips.

"Why are you out of bed? The coffee is almost done."

"Your mom has summoned us over to Nathan's house within an hour."

"What? Why? Did you tell her no?"

"I'm not telling your mother no. Feel free to call her yourself and tell her we're not coming." Her brow arched.

"Why do we have to go over to Nathan's?"

"She didn't say. We better take a shower together to save time." Her tongue ran over her lips.

"I'm right behind you, baby." I grinned.

175

CHAPTER 43

*M*ason

When the cab pulled up to Nathan's house, we saw my mother standing on the steps of his porch.

"Why is she just standing there like that?" Sara asked.

"I haven't got a clue. Let's go find out." I opened the door, and we both climbed out.

"Good, you made it." My mother smiled.

"Like we had a choice. Why are you just standing out here?" I asked.

"I want to show you something. Follow me." We followed her down the steps and to the townhome that was next door.

She slid the key in the lock and opened the door, motioning for us to go inside.

"Mother, what is going on? Did you buy this place?"

"I did. What do you think?"

I silently snickered because she'd be living right next door to Nathan. The thought excited me.

"Caitlin, this is beautiful. What about your other townhome?" Sara asked.

"This isn't for me, darling. It's for the two of you. Welcome to your new home," she said.

"What?" I glanced at her in shock.

"I bought this place because it was too good of a deal to pass up and you were taking too long to decide. I wasn't about to let it slip out from under you. Look around and envision all the changes you can make."

"Mom. I can't believe you did this." I kissed her cheek.

"I've been saving it for the right time, and the right time has come. The deed to the house is in your name. I paid cash for it so you can pay me back in monthly installments, interest free."

"I don't know what to say." I wrapped my arms around her and gave her a hug. "Thank you so much. I love you."

"I love you too, and I know you both will be very happy here. Now, I need to get to the office." She dropped the keys to the house in my hand and placed her hand on my cheek. "Enjoy your new home." She softly smiled.

"I can't believe your Mom did this," Sara spoke as she looked around.

"I can't either." I hooked my arm around her. "It needs some work."

"Yeah. It does need updated, but it's still perfect."

"Well, what do you think?" I heard Nathan's voice from behind.

Turning around, I saw him standing in the doorway with a grin on his face.

"We love it, bro. I can't believe Mom did this."

"I can. She wanted you nice and close to her." He grinned.

"Shit. That's right. She's just right around the block."

"Yep, and she loves to pop in unexpectedly way too much."

Six Months Later

*W*e finally completed the remodel on our townhome, and everything worked out perfectly. Sara and I picked everything together. From the cabinets, countertops, moldings, fixtures, flooring and every piece of furniture to fill our new home.

"This is the last box," I spoke as I set it down on the floor.

"Everything turned out perfect." Sara smiled as she stood in our newly renovated kitchen.

"You're perfect." I wrapped my arms around her from behind.

"No. You're perfect," she spoke.

"I think you're more perfect." I kissed the top of her head.

"Okay, you two knock it off. We all know you're both perfect." Elijah smirked as he and Aspen walked in with Mila.

"Aspen, I'm so happy you're here. I can't wait to show you what we did upstairs," Sara excitedly spoke as they walked out of the kitchen.

"This looks great, bro. You two did a magnificent job."

"Thanks." I patted his back.

"What's wrong?" he asked. "You have that look."

"Nothing's wrong. Absolutely nothing. You and Nathan were right."

"About what?"

"About being in love. I thought I was happy being a bachelor, but I really never was."

"You grew up, little brother." He smiled. "Welcome to adulthood."

"Hello, hello." I heard my mother's voice and Elijah let out a chuckle.

"Better you than me," he said.

*T*wo months after Sara came back from California, we got word that Jack had passed away. My mother had his body flown back to New York, and we gave him a proper burial as a family. Sara and I would occasionally visit his grave site where we would put down fresh flowers. He died alone, and a part of me felt bad for him.

Nobody should have to die all alone. But it was the choice he made when he left New York. As angry as I was throughout the years, I was happy I got the chance to know him, even if it was for a short time. Nathan was neutral about the situation, and Elijah still harbored some resentment. But overall, our family was stronger than ever.

EPILOGUE

Two Years Later

Over the past two years, there had been some big changes to our family. Elijah and Aspen welcomed their second child, a son, whom they named Carter Charles Wolfe, after our grandfather. Nathan and Allison finally got married and nine months later, their daughter, Aurora Victoria Wolfe, entered the world. A couple months after Sara and I moved into the townhouse, I proposed to her and she graciously accepted. Our family, that was made up of just the four of us, was growing fast, and it made my mother incredibly happy.

Sara finally completed her fellowship and had officially become a trauma surgeon at Lenox Hill Hospital. With that out of the way, it was time to plan our wedding, something I had been looking forward to for the past two years. Six months later, she finally became Mrs. Mason Wolfe, and I was the happiest man alive.

"I love you, Mrs. Wolfe." I grinned as I brushed my lips against her.

"I love you too, Mr. Wolfe."

After our ceremony, and before we headed to the reception, we went to Central Park to take some pictures.

"Everyone please gather around the fountain with Mason and Sara standing in the middle," our photographer spoke.

We did as she asked as she told us to smile while she snapped our family photo. A photo that would hang on the wall in each of our homes to remind us how precious our family is.

My brothers and I stood back for a moment while everyone else headed towards their limos to go to the reception. It was only the three of us, just like it used to be before our women walked into our lives.

"Look at us. All the Wolfe brothers are married. Did you ever think we'd be standing here together as married men?" Elijah asked.

"I had my doubts." Nathan smirked.

"Never. But I'm happy we are. I couldn't imagine my life without Sara."

"I couldn't imagine my life without Aspen and the kids."

"I couldn't imagine my life without Allison and the kids."

"I can still imagine my life without kids for the moment." I grinned.

Elijah sighed as he placed his hand on my shoulder. "Just wait, little brother. Your time will come soon and then we'll all be standing somewhere in this park together as fathers."

*E*lijah was right. A year later, Sara gave birth to our son, Wyatt Jackson Wolfe. As we gathered in Central Park for our annual family picnic, the three of us stood with a drink in our hand as we watched our children. A new generation of the Wolfe family had emerged, and the start of a new legacy was born.

Get a sneak peek of the first two chapters of LOGAN (A Hockey Romance) on the next page.

LOGAN

Blurb

Logan

I was one of the best players in the NHL and as fast as lightning on the ice. Hockey was my life. It consumed me. It was the one thing I could commit to. I was a bachelor—happy and living the ultimate dream. Then the accident happened, and the doctors told me I'd never play hockey again. My life went to hell in the blink of an eye. All hope and the will to live was gone: until Brooke Alexander walked into my life.

Brooke

I was hired to help Logan Jackson get back on the ice. I had rules. Rules he needed to follow if he was going to play hockey again. He was stubborn, defiant, and nothing I couldn't handle. Rehabilitation was going to be difficult and pure hell. I had to break him in order to help him. I knew what it was like to have your dreams taken away from you, and I was determined to give him his dream back, even if it meant losing him.

CHAPTER 1

*L*ogan

"He shoots and he scores!"

The crowd cheered as I skated around the ice with a wide grin and my stick proudly held up in the air. The adrenaline that rushed through me never got old. The first game of the season and three goals, shot by yours truly, bringing home the win for our team. My teammates gathered around me; wild beasts throwing their bodies around in excitement at the victory that was ours. Screams filled the arena. I scanned the crowd, but the only thing I could focus on was how my dad wasn't there to watch me. Skating off the ice, the team headed to the locker room where champagne sprayed all over us, celebrating our win.

"You're fast and furious, bro," my best friend and teammate, Tommy, said.

"Thanks, Tommy. We all played a great game tonight."

Our coach, Gene Young, entered the locker room with a wide grin on his face.

"Excellent game, boys. I'm proud of each and every one of you. Practice tomorrow at eight a.m. sharp. Our next game is with the L.A.

Kings and I want to blow those sons of bitches out of the water. Losing isn't an option. Understand?"

"Yes, coach," we all spoke as he walked out of the locker room.

There was much celebrating to do and we were about to head out to Louie's Bar. Grabbing my bag, I walked out of the locker room where my two brothers, Brandon and Owen, were leaning up against the wall.

"Great game, bro." Owen fist-bumped me.

"You were amazing out there tonight. I'm so proud of you." Brandon smiled as he patted my shoulder.

"Where's Dad?" I asked with a hint of disappointment.

"I'm sure he was passed out drunk somewhere," Brandon spoke.

I didn't know why disappointment shadowed inside me. He rarely attended my games, and when he did, he was usually drunk before he showed up.

"Forget about him." Owen hooked his arm around me. "Let's go find some girls and get laid tonight."

As we walked into Louie's Bar, the team was already sitting down at our usual table. Taking our seats, I grabbed the bottle of beer that was already waiting for me.

"To the amazing Lightning Logan." Beer bottles clanked together.

That was what they called me, Lightning Logan, because I was as quick as lightning on the ice. I was introduced to hockey when I was six years old when my dad took me to my very first game. From that moment on, becoming an NHL hockey player consumed me. It was my life and all the hard work I'd put into it paid off. I was scouted by the New York Rangers at the age of seventeen when I played for my high school team and took us to the nationals. Scoring three goals in under a minute and being the fastest player on the ice snagged me a place on the team with a starting salary and contract that nearly gave me a heart attack. A year after proving my value, consecutive wins and scoring the goal that won us the Stanley Cup with four seconds left in the game, I was endorsed by Nike, Gillette, Coca Cola, and Polo Ralph Lauren, bringing me into the top ten highest paid endorsed athletes in the world.

I had it all. Fame, fortune, and pretty much any woman I wanted. Dating to me was an occasional dinner and sex. Or most of the time, just sex. There were a lot of one-night stands, especially when we played away games. Relationships and commitments were a definite no for me. I was already in a committed relationship and it was with hockey. The one and only love of my life. I'd watched some of my teammates with their girlfriends and it never worked out. The arguing and the constant jealousy were always at the forefront of their relationships. I didn't have time for that shit, nor did I want it. I was happy being a bachelor, doing a job I loved more than anything in the world and fucking beautiful women, knowing they'd be gone the next morning.

After kicking back another beer, I got up to use the restroom. When I was finished, I walked out and saw a pretty girl who stood about five feet four with long black hair leaning up against the wall.

"Hey." She smiled. "Aren't you Logan Jackson from the New York Rangers?"

"Hi, and yes, I am." I politely smiled back.

"I was at the game and you were amazing out there." She bit her bottom lip.

Placing my hands in my pockets, I spoke, "Thank you."

"Today's my twenty-first birthday and the tickets were a present from my friends. They know how much I love hockey."

She had a great smile and big brown eyes. I needed to celebrate my win and she was just the girl to help me with that.

"Since it's your birthday and your twenty-first, let me buy you a drink."

"Thank you. That would be great."

"What's your name?"

"Tori."

"Nice to meet you, Tori." I extended my hand to her.

When I walked back to the table to tell the guys I was sitting up at the bar with Tori, my brother, Owen, lightly took hold of my arm and pulled me into the corner.

"Way to go, bro." He smiled.

"It's her twenty-first birthday and I'm just buying her a drink to celebrate her legal drinking age." I winked.

"Have fun tapping that ass." He patted me on the back before he and Brandon left the bar.

❧

The rustling of the sheets and a low moan awoke me from a sound sleep. I lay there frozen, trying to remember my actions from last night. My head hurt. Too many beers followed by several shots of tequila really did me in. The only thing I remembered was her screaming out my name multiple times.

"Morning," she whispered in my ear as she placed her hand on my shoulder.

"Morning," I mumbled.

"I had the best time last night and the best birthday ever."

"I'm happy you had a nice birthday." I got up from the bed and went into the bathroom. "I have practice in a couple of hours, so I think it's best if you got dressed and headed home. I can call you a cab."

I threw on a pair of sweatpants and headed to the kitchen to make a pot of coffee.

"Are you serious?" she asked as she emerged from the bedroom.

"Serious about what?"

"About me leaving. I thought maybe last night meant something. I mean, it just seemed like we had a connection."

Shit. She was one of those girls. I rolled my eyes before I turned around and looked into her sad puppy eyes.

"Listen, Tori. You're a great girl and all, but last night was just a one-time thing. We both drank too much and had some fun. I'm pretty sure I'm not the only one-night stand you've had."

The sadness in her eyes turned to rage. "Actually, you are. I don't do this kind of thing. I'm not that kind of girl."

"Then why did you do it with me?" I asked nonchalantly.

"Because I felt something when we first met, and I got the vibe that you felt it too. I guess I was wrong," she spoke as she slipped her feet into her heels. "You may be a good fuck, but you're a total asshole, and you know what? Karma is a bitch." She stormed out the door, slamming it behind her.

I sighed as I poured myself a cup of coffee. Walking into the bathroom to take a shower, I heard my phone beep with a text message from Owen.

"How was that chick last night?"

"I don't really remember. But she just left all pissed off and called me an asshole."

"Lightning Logan strikes again. Anyway, you're going to dinner at Dad's tonight, right?"

"Shit. Is that tonight?"

"Yep. Seven o'clock."

"Why is he having us over for dinner anyway?"

"Apparently, he met someone, and he wants to introduce us to her."

"Fuck. You have got to be kidding."

"Nope, bro. Just be there and try to be nice."

"I can't make any promises."

The feeling in the pit of my stomach wasn't a good one. Whoever this woman was, I hoped she knew what she was getting herself into. Anger ripped through me and the only way I knew how to deal with it was taking it out on the ice.

CHAPTER 2

*L*ogan

    I started my warmup with some diagonal dribbles, increasing my speed until I was at full force around the ice before moving the puck from side to side. I started practice on my own before the rest of the team arrived.

"Hey," Tommy shouted from the other side of the wall. "Are you ready for me?"

Looking up at him with a smile, I spoke, "Bring it on, bitch."

He furiously skated out on the ice, heading towards me with his stick in position, ready to steal the puck out from under me. Moving my stick from side to side, protecting the puck in every way possible, I shot it across the ice as Tommy and I raced for it.

"Dude, you're on fire today. What's up?" he asked as his stick stole the puck.

"Going to my dad's for dinner. I guess he met someone."

"Is that a good thing?" We battled for the puck.

"I'm not sure yet." Our sticks tangled and I stole the puck.

"It's been eighteen years, dude. It's about time your old man went out and met someone."

"Eighteen drunken years. I wonder if she knows he's an alcoholic."

"Guess you'll find out tonight."

Coach Gene and the rest of the team skated out on the ice as he told us to line up for conditioning.

"Okay, listen up, boys. Tomorrow night, we play against the Washington Capitals on our turf. I don't want any mishaps with them like last season. I know some of you have problems with the players, but for the sake of the game, keep it clean. They won their first game of the season like us. Let's not let them win their second game. When you're done conditioning, I want to go over some new plays for tomorrow night. Now let's get moving."

About thirty minutes into practice, the coach called me off the ice.

"What's up, coach?"

"I'm putting you on warning right now for tomorrow's game. That little stunt you pulled last season with Gavin Machard cost us the win of the game, not to mention the fact that he was out all season rehabilitating the knee you broke."

"He came at me first." I pointed my finger at him.

"Doesn't matter. You broke the kid's knee and cost him the season and us the game. Stay away from him. Do you understand me? You're the best player on this team. Shit, you're pretty much the best player in the whole damn league. Don't fuck it up, because I will pull you from the game."

"No you won't. You need me and you know it. Without me on this team, we wouldn't be where we are today."

"You're a cocky son of a bitch, Logan. Now get back out there and finish practice."

"I don't need practice, coach." I winked as I skated back onto the ice.

❧

Upon exiting my building, Ollie, my brother Brandon's driver, opened the door.

"Good evening, Logan." He politely smiled.

"Good evening, Ollie." I smiled back as I climbed in next to my brother. "Where's Owen?" I asked, as I didn't see him.

"He's going to meet us there. He had something to do."

"I swear to God, if he bails, I'm kicking his ass."

Brandon chuckled. "He's not bailing and I'm sure he would kick *your* ass, little brother."

Pulling up to my childhood home, I sighed. "Are Aunt Vanessa and Uncle Alan coming?"

"I don't think Dad invited them. I believe it's just us."

Climbing out of the limo, my stomach twisted in a knot at the fact that I had to face my father who couldn't bring himself to my first game last night. When we walked into the house, he greeted us at the door, shaking Brandon's hand first. I walked away and went into the kitchen to grab a beer before he had the chance to say anything to me. Opening the refrigerator, I noticed there wasn't any.

"Good to see you, Logan," my father spoke as he walked into the kitchen with Brandon. "I'm sorry I couldn't come to your game last night."

"Yeah. Whatever, Dad. So where is this woman you so badly want us to meet?"

"I'm right here." A woman who stood approximately five foot five answered as she entered the kitchen.

My father walked over and hooked his arm around her. "Boys, I'd like you to meet Maggie. Maggie, these are two of my boys, Brandon, CEO of Jackson Software, and Logan, professional hockey player for the New York Rangers."

She extended her hand to Brandon first and then to me. I lightly shook it.

"It's nice to finally meet both of you. Your father has told me so much about you."

Rolling my eyes, I turned and opened the liquor cabinet. It was empty. Before I could ask about it, the front door opened, and Owen walked in.

"Now that everyone is here, let's sit down to dinner," my father spoke as he placed his hand on the small of her back and led her to the table.

Maggie was an attractive woman. She wore her blonde hair in a short bob-cut style that complemented her green eyes. She looked around the same age as my dad, fifty-eight. Maybe a year or two younger.

"Dad, where's the beer?" I asked.

"There isn't any."

I narrowed my eye and arched my brow at him. "What?"

"I've quit drinking," he spoke.

I chuckled. "Yeah, right. Seriously, where is it?"

"I'm not joking, son. I haven't mentioned this to you boys yet because I haven't seen you in a while, but I've stopped drinking and I've been going to AA meetings. That's why I couldn't go to your game last night. I had a meeting."

I looked over at Brandon and Owen, who had the same expression on their faces that I did.

"In fact, that is where I met Maggie. She's my sponsor." He reached over and placed his hand on hers.

"That's great, Dad," Brandon spoke.

"So let me get this straight." I placed my napkin on the table. "You decide after eighteen years to give up the booze and then you date your sponsor? Isn't there some rule against that?"

"No. There's no rule against that," he replied.

"And how long have you been sober, Maggie?"

"Five years." She smiled.

"Maggie and I have been seeing each other for the past couple of months. She's great support and we enjoy each other's company."

Shaking my head, I got up from the table.

"Logan!" my father shouted. "Sit down and finish the dinner that Maggie so kindly prepared for us." He pointed at me.

"You don't get to tell me what to do, old man. You haven't done that in eighteen years and now you think you're going to start? Fuck you!"

My father got up from his seat. "You will not use that kind of language in my house and especially not in front of Maggie. If you can't show some respect, then get out!"

"Don't worry. I am." I stormed out of the dining room and out the front door. Before too long, Brandon and Owen were by my side.

"Bro, what the fuck is the matter with you?" Owen spoke as he grabbed my arm. "She seems nice and Dad quit drinking. Doesn't that count for something?"

"Whatever, Owen. Go back and be a happy family. Forgive that bastard for the things he's done over the past eighteen years. Maybe you can forget about it, but I can't." I jerked away from him and started walking down the street. Placing my hands in my pockets, I turned around. "Ask yourself why you got into boxing in the first place, bro. You have just as much anger towards him as I do."

When I reached the corner, I made a right turn and headed to Dewey's Bar. Sitting on the stool, Lina, the bartender I'd known for a couple of years, placed a beer in front of me.

"You look like you could use this, Logan."

"Thanks, Lina."

After my mom died, when I was nine years old, the only way my father could handle her death was to drink himself into oblivion every night. The minute he came home from work, when he did come home, he'd pop open a beer and sit in his chair in front of the TV, ignoring the fact that he even had three sons. His sister, my Aunt Vanessa, ended up caring for me and my brothers after my father started heavily drinking. She made sure we went to school and she put us on the right path to our careers, never letting us stray or go off course. I owed my life to her because she was the one who made sure I had every opportunity available to me when it came to hockey. She and her husband, my Uncle Alan, provided the things my father couldn't. It pained her to see her brother's life go to shit, and as many times as she tried to help him, she always failed. He was a shit father who only cared about his alcohol, forgetting the fact that he wasn't the only one who lost someone he loved.

As I took a swig of my beer, my mind went back to my thirteenth birthday. For some reason, I thought maybe that would be the one night he wouldn't come home drunk. But he did. My aunt had just set my birthday cake on the table and he was late as usual. When he walked in and saw us all sitting down at the table, he went into a rage, yelling and screaming about how inconsiderate we were not to have waited for him. He picked the cake up from the table and threw it across the kitchen. I remember the anger that consumed me at that moment, and I lunged at him, punching him across the face. He grabbed me and threw me up against the wall, screaming at me and telling me that I was nothing but a punk kid who would never amount to anything. That was the night I ran away and hit the rink, skating the fastest I ever had around ice. It was that night that I was determined to show my father he was wrong and that I would become something and someone.

"You ready for another?" Lina asked with a smile.

"Yeah." I handed her my empty beer bottle.

I couldn't help but stare at her tits as her tight black low-cut shirt embraced them. She was thirty-five, smoking hot, and always flirting with me when I'd come in, which wasn't too often since I rarely visited my father.

"I watched the game last night," she spoke as she handed me another beer. "You were great."

"Thanks. I'm also great at other things." I winked.

"I bet you are." She bit down on her bottom lip as she leaned over the bar.

My eyes diverted to her sweet cleavage and then up at her. "Do you want to find out?"

"Yeah. Actually, I do." She looked at her watch. "Look at that. It's time for my break." She smiled. "Hey, Joe. I'm going on break."

She motioned for me to follow her down a long hallway and into a room that housed a desk and a couple of filing cabinets. After I entered, she shut and locked the door, then lifted her shirt over her head, exposing her black bra that looked too small for her big tits. Grabbing her hands, I pushed her up against the wall and held her arms above her head with one hand. Her teeth nipped at my bottom lip while my hand traveled up her skirt and my fingers pushed her silk panties to the side and plunged deep inside her. She moaned and I let go of her wrists.

"Take off your bra and show me your tits."

She reached behind her and unhooked it, taking the straps down, and letting it fall to the ground. My lips explored her bare breasts as her hands worked on my pants, taking them down and releasing my throbbing cock.

"Nice dick." She smiled.

After removing my fingers from her wet pussy, I told her to turn around and face the wall. Pulling a condom from my wallet, I slipped it on and crammed myself inside her. She gasped and let out several low grunts as I pounded into her fast and furiously.

"Is this what you wanted?" I asked.

"Yes. Oh yes," she moaned.

I reached around and grabbed hold of her tits, pinching her nipples as her pussy swelled around me, and her body tightened as a wave of warmth rushed over my cock, causing me to come.

"Ah, yeah. Fuck yeah," I moaned.

Pulling out of her, I rolled the condom off and pulled up my pants.

"What do you want me to do with this?" I asked.

"I'll throw it away in the trash up at the bar. I don't want the boss to know that I fuck in here." She smiled. "You want another beer?"

"Nah. I'm going to head home. Thanks, Lina. I needed that."

"No problem, Logan. You sure know how to satisfy a woman."

I gave her a small smile as I walked out of the office and out of the bar.

Click the link below to download your copy of LOGAN!
Amazon Universal Link: mybook.to/LOGAN

BOOKS BY SANDI LYNN

If you haven't already done so, please check out my other books. Escape from reality and into the world of romance. I'll take you on a journey of love, pain, heartache and happily ever afters.

Millionaires:

The Forever Series (Forever Black, Forever You, Forever Us, Being Julia, Collin, A Forever Christmas, A Forever Family)

Love, Lust & A Millionaire (Wyatt Brothers, Book 1)

Love, Lust & Liam (Wyatt Brothers, Book 2)

Lie Next To Me (A Millionaire's Love, Book 1)

When I Lie with You (A Millionaire's Love, Book 2)

Then You Happened (Happened Series, Book 1)

Then We Happened (Happened Series, Book 2)

His Proposed Deal

A Love Called Simon

The Seduction of Alex Parker

Something About Lorelei

One Night In London

The Exception

Corporate A$$ETS

A Beautiful Sight

The Negotiation

Defense

Playing The Millionaire

#Delete

Behind His Lies

Carter Grayson (Redemption Series, Book One)

Chase Calloway (Redemption Series, Book Two)

Jamieson Finn (Redemption Series, Book Three)

Damien Prescott (Redemption Series, Book Four)

The Interview: New York & Los Angeles Part 1

The Interview: New York & Los Angeles Part 2

One Night In Paris

Perfectly You

The Escort

The Ring

Elijah Wolfe (Wolfe Brothers Series, Book One)

Nathan Wolfe (Wolfe Brothers Series, Book Two)

Mason Wolfe (Wolfe Brothers Series, Book Three)

The Donor

Second Chance Love:

Rewind

Remembering You

When I'm With You

Love In Between (Love Series, Book 1)

The Upside of Love (Love Series, Book 2)

Sports:

LOGAN (A Hockey Romance)

ABOUT THE AUTHOR

Sandi Lynn is a *New York Times, USA Today* and *Wall Street Journal* bestselling author who spends all her days writing. She published her first novel, *Forever Black*, in February 2013 and hasn't stopped writing since. Her mission is to provide readers with romance novels that will whisk them away to another world and from the daily grind of life – one book at a time.

Be a part of my tribe and make sure to sign up for my newsletter so you don't miss a Sandi Lynn book again!

Website
Newsletter
Goodreads
Bookbub

Printed in Great Britain
by Amazon

52413275R00119